SPECIAL MESSAGE TO READERS

This book is published by
THE ULVERSCROFT FOUNDATION,
a registered charity in the U.K., No. 264873

The Foundation was established in 1974 to provide funds to help towards research, diagnosis and treatment of eye diseases. Below are a few examples of contributions made by THE ULVERSCROFT FOUNDATION:

★ A new Children's Assessment Unit at Moorfield's Hospital, London.

★ Twin operating theatres at the Western Ophthalmic Hospital, London.

★ The Frederick Thorpe Ulverscroft Chair of Ophthalmology at the University of Leicester.

★ Eye Laser equipment to various eye hospitals.

If you would like to help further the work of the Foundation by making a donation or leaving a legacy, every contribution, no matter how small, is received with gratitude. Please write for details to:

THE ULVERSCROFT FOUNDATION,
The Green, Bradgate Road, Anstey,
Leicestershire, LE7 7FU. England.
Telephone: (0533) 364325

Love is
a time of enchantment:
in it all days are fair and all fields
green. Youth is blest by it,
old age made benign: the eyes of love see
roses blooming in December,
and sunshine through rain. Verily
is the time of true-love
a time of enchantment—and
Oh! how eager is woman
to be bewitched!

JOURNEY INTO DANGER

Learning she is to inherit her grandfather's estate Rachel travels to meet her new relations—her grandfather's second wife, and her son, Philip. She also meets the forbidding Jason Holcroft. She falls in love and everything seems set fair. Instead she finds fear and danger. Who can she trust? Philip or Jason? Before she finds the answer her life is endangered. But at last she wins through to love and happiness.

BEATRICE TAYLOR

JOURNEY INTO DANGER

Complete and Unabridged

ULVERSCROFT
Leicester

First published in Great Britain in 1973 by
Robert Hale Ltd.,
London

First Large Print Edition
published September 1989

British Library CIP Data

Taylor, Beatrice–
Journey into danger.—Large print ed.—
Ulverscroft large print series: romance, suspense
I. Title
823′.914[F]

ISBN 0-7089-2063-2

Published by
F. A. Thorpe (Publishing) Ltd.
Anstey, Leicestershire
Set by Rowland Phototypesetting Ltd.
Bury St. Edmunds, Suffolk
Printed and bound in Great Britain by
T. J. Press (Padstow) Ltd., Padstow, Cornwall

1

"**R**ACHEL!"

I had been sitting beside the low fire, half asleep in the rocking chair, hidden by a screen from Mama, but almost before that low whisper reached me I was at her side.

"I'm here, Mama." I turned the shaded lamp on the table so that more light shone on the bed. "Are you ready for your cordial?"

"No, I don't want it yet."

I took one of her thin hands in mine, trying not to sound as worried as I felt, because they were so wasted there seemed no longer any flesh on them.

"It will do you good," I said coaxingly. "You know the doctor said—"

"No. It makes me sleepy and then I can't—Rachel, I must talk to you tonight. I'll have it afterwards. It won't matter then."

I looked down at her dear face, almost whiter than the pillow on which her head

1

rested, and felt a stab of real fear, admitting to myself for the first time that Mama was getting weaker every day; was slowly wasting away.

My fingers tightened convulsively on hers at that thought and she gave a little whimper of pain. Hard though it was to do so, I buried my fears deep and tried to be cheerful, though I alone knew what it cost me.

"All right, dearest. Only don't tire yourself too much."

"It doesn't matter now." I had to bend my head to catch the whispered words. "There's a letter under the pillow. Find it and read it to me."

I hesitated, thinking for an alarmed moment that Mama's mind was beginning to wander. Then as she moved her head impatiently I bent and felt underneath the pillow, withdrawing my hand after a moment's search, the envelope between my fingers.

"You've found it?"

"Yes, Mama. When did it come?"

"This morning while you were taking your walk. But that doesn't matter. Open it. Be quick, my love."

I did as she asked, ripping the envelope and drawing out the letter with suddenly trembling fingers.

"Read it," came the impatient whisper from the bed.

"It's from a lawyer, Mama—"

"I know that. Read it quickly. There isn't much time."

Again I felt that painful stab of fear but I tried to keep my voice calm and give no indication of my troubled thoughts as I began to read.

"Dear Madam, I acknowledge your belated letter in answer to my advertisement, regarding your daughter, Rachel Mary Morley. I hope to call on you next Thursday morning to discuss this matter at about midday. Will you please have the proofs of your marriage and your daughter's parentage ready for my inspection."

My voice died away and I stared at the letter in my hand, hardly able to understand it.

"That's in three days' time. Mama, what does it mean? What advertisement is he talking about?"

3

"Get the deed box out of the basket trunk, Rachel."

I got up, the heavy skirt of my dress brushing against the end of the bed as I passed it and billowing around my feet as I bent to lift the deed box out of the trunk. Then I took it to the bed, putting it down on the table.

"Here it is, Mama. Shall I open it?"

There was no answer and my heart leaped into my throat. I lifted the lamp and leaned over the bed, fearing the worst. But as the light shone on her Mama stirred and said faintly:

"Yes, open it, my love."

Fighting down my renewed fears I turned the key which was already in the lock and lifted back the lid, seeing immediately the newspaper cutting, reading it with complete disbelief.

"Morley," it was headed. "If Edward Tobias Morley or any of his issue will write to the undersigned, he may hear something to his advantage."

It was signed by the lawyer whose letter I had just read out.

"Edward Tobias Morley? That's Papa, isn't it? When—"

4

"Yes. The housekeeper where I worked saw it. She pointed it out to me. 'Here you are, Morley,' she said. 'Try that. Maybe somebody's left you a fortune.' Then she laughed and went away."

Her voice faded in an exhausted way and I said urgently:

"Mama, let me give you your cordial."

"No. Not yet."

"Then take a little warm milk. Please, Mama—"

"Very well."

Quickly I went to the fireplace where I had put the milk to heat on the hob and carefully poured it into a cup. I stirred in a little honey then went back to the bed, lifting Mama until she was resting against me.

"Now, dearest, drink it all up. It will do you good."

I put the cup to her lips and was relieved when she drank almost all of it. Then I laid her back on the pillow and drew up the bedclothes around her.

"That's better. Now rest for a minute."

"There's no time." There was so much urgency in her exhausted voice that I said no more, feeling again that surge of fear.

5

"I didn't write then. Not until we came here and I knew—Rachel, my marriage lines and all our birth certifcates are in the box. Lock it up and put the key on your locket chain. Wear it inside your dress for safety."

"Yes, Mama, but why—?"

"Do it now."

Without another word I took off the gold chain which I always wore, carrying the locket with the miniatures of Mama and Papa. I put the key on to it, then undid the tiny buttons of the fitted bodice of my dress and pushed the locket and key inside.

"I've done it, Mama," I said quietly.

"That's well, my love. When this lawyer comes show him everything but don't let him take them away."

"Why not, Mama?"

"Because they're all you've got to prove who you are. Promise me you'll do as I say, Rachel. Promise!"

"I promise," I said steadily.

"Good. Now I'll have that cordial."

I hesitated, wanting to ask all the questions which were crowding into my mind, but looking at that worn face on the

6

pillow, I knew I must not. I would have to wait until tomorrow when she was more rested.

I administered the cordial to her, then kissed her and stayed beside her, holding her hand in mine, until the opiate began to take effect.

When she was sleeping quietly I went back to the rocking chair by the fire, putting on more coal piece by piece so that I would not disturb her. Then I sat down and rocked myself backwards and forwards gently, while I thought and wondered about the advertisement and the letter I had just read.

I do not know when I drifted from thought into sleep, nor do I know what roused me an hour or so later. I only knew as I hurried to the bed and looked down at Mama, lying there so peacefully with a faint smile on her lips, that while I had slept she had slipped away.

She had left me without a farewell, without any real warning.

I sank down beside the bed and buried my face in my hands, crying painfully but without sound. Because now, at the age of nineteen, I was utterly alone in the world.

With both mother and father dead there was nobody to whom I could turn; nobody whom I could call my own.

The next two days passed like a bad dream, made bearable only by the kindness of the doctor who had attended Mama and by our landlady, both of whom went with me to the quiet funeral which was held on the morning of the third day.

I was in the sitting-room, trying to concentrate on what I was going to do in the future, when Mrs. Corner, the landlady, came in and said respectfully: "There's a gentleman called, Miss, asking for your mother. He says he's from a lawyer."

"A gentleman for Mama? But—" I stopped, remembering for the first time the letter I had read to Mama the night she died and what she had told me to do.

"Will you see him, Miss?"

"Yes," I said with difficulty. "I must."

I got up and went to stand by the fireplace, feeling very young and afraid even though I was wearing my red hair which had been such a cross to me all my life drawn severely into a knot at the back of

8

my head, and had on my plainest and darkest dress.

The man who came in a moment later hesitated in the doorway, his height suddenly making the room seem much smaller by comparison, and looked at me, his thick black brows drawing together in a frown.

"I've called to see Mrs. Mary Morley. Where is she?" he asked brusquely.

"She isn't here," I answered and then was vexed with myself for making such a stupidly obvious reply.

"Then perhaps you'll be good enough to tell her I've called."

It was fortunate for me at that moment that this big, black-browed and black-haired man whose deep voice was curt almost to the point of rudeness, aroused me to annoyance, otherwise I might not have been able to restrain my tears at the thought that never again would I be able to speak to Mama.

How dared he look at me in that arrogant way and talk to me as if I was some little maidservant who did not know her place?

And the lost and lonely feeling which

had been with me since Mama died disappeared in the wave of anger which swept over me.

He frowned even more formidably.

"Do you hear me? Who are you?" he asked.

I drew myself up to my full height which was not very much at the best of times being barely five foot two, and said in a dignified way:

"I am Miss Rachel Mary Morley."

"You? Mrs. Morley's daughter? But you're only a child."

"I am not! I'm nineteen!" I said indignantly, ruffled as I always am when because of my pale skin and slight build I am taken for younger than my years.

He lifted his brows.

"Are you? I wouldn't have thought it." He looked at me in silence for a minute, his deep-set brown eyes roaming indifferently over my face and figure, and to my added annoyance I felt the hot colour flame into my cheeks. "Where is your mother?"

"Dead," I said, and with that word all my sorrow at my loss swept over me again, ousting the anger this arrogant man had roused in me.

"Dead?" he repeated, looking very taken aback. "When?"

"Three days since. She was buried this morning."

I moved then, sitting down in the chair I had recently vacated, turning my face away from him so that he would not see my tears.

"I'm sorry. I had no idea. You're not wearing mourning."

"I have none, nor money to buy it. Anyway, neither Papa nor Mama believed in—in trappings, so—"

"Please accept my condolences," he said, briefly and very formally and I, who did not want expressions of sympathy from anybody and particularly from this man, in my usual contrary way felt upset because of his curt, unfeeling manner.

"Thank you," I answered and looked at him again, seeing an expression of frowning concentration on his face.

"May I sit down?"

I nodded, vexed with myself because I had not thought to ask him to do so, but determined that I would not apologize for my lack of good manners.

He took the chair opposite to me, his big frame completely filling it, and stretched out his long trousered legs.

"Do you know why I've come?"

"Yes. Mama answered an advertisement. A lawyer wrote to say he would come today to see her. Was it you?"

He shook his head.

"No. Lacey was taken ill yesterday and asked me to come in his place."

"Then who are you?"

"I'm sorry. I should have introduced myself. I am Jason Holcroft. I lived at Clifton Manor for many years."

"Clifton Manor?"

"Tobias Morley's residence. Your Grandfather, presumably, if you can prove your claim. You have documents?"

"I have my parents' marriage lines and our birth certificates."

"Let me see them," he commanded.

I looked across at him, sitting very straight in my chair.

"Why should I? How do I know what right you have to look at them?"

He smiled slightly.

"A good question. I'm glad you've enough sense to ask it. Here are my credentials."

He put his hand inside his coat and handed me a letter. I opened it and read it deliberately, irritated by his patronizing words about my "sense" and determined to let him see that even though I might be young, I was not exactly stupid.

It was signed by the lawyer who had written to Mama and introduced Jason Holcroft Esquire as his agent.

"Excuse me," I said and got up. "I'll get the documents."

I went into the room next door and took the deed box out of the basket trunk, standing holding it for a few minutes while I fought the bereft feeling which always overcame me at the sight of the empty bed, its covers drawn neatly over it, where Mama had died.

Then I pulled my gold chain and locket over my head and went back into the sitting-room. There I unlocked the box, took out the certificates, and handed them to him.

He examined them carefully before saying curtly:

"These appear to be in order. I'll take them to Lacey and—"

"No, you will not," I interrupted. "Give them back to me at once."

He looked at me as if he could not believe his ears, and if I had not been so afraid at the angry glint in his eyes I believe I must have laughed. Because from his expression it seemed as if this was the first time anybody had ever crossed him.

"How dare you?" he said at last. "Are you accusing me of being a thief? A scoundrel?"

In spite of my fear of him I put up my chin in the way Mama had always deplored and said steadily:

"No, I'm not. But Mama told me not to let the papers out of my own hands because they're all I've got to prove who I am."

He smiled then, though grimly, but it was amazing the difference it made to his dark face. But it was only fleeting and when he spoke it was still in the same hard, sharp way.

"You're mistaken, Miss Morley. You carry proofs of your paternity in your hair and face."

14

I frowned, not liking that personal remark.

"I don't know what you mean."

"Why, that you're very like old Tobias Morley, that's all, and presumably like your father. Didn't you know?"

"That I'm like Papa? Yes, I suppose so. Mama said his hair used to be my colour but I only remember it snow white."

"White? But he was only a young man, surely?"

I nodded.

"He was not yet forty when he died, but something happened, I don't know what, that made his hair turn white." I picked up the locket from the table and opened it. "Look. Here are my parents."

I handed it to him and he studied the miniatures closely.

"These pictures are small and not very clear, but there's definitely a family like-ness," he said at last. "Keep the locket safely, and the papers. Take good care of them. At Clifton Manor—"

He stopped and I stared at him, puzzled and surprised by the serious way in which he had spoken. I waited for him to continue, and when he did not speak again, said quietly:

"I wear the locket and chain always. Can I have the papers back, please?"

He started, as if his mind had been somewhere else.

"Yes, of course. After all, I know of no reason why you should trust me."

"No." I took the papers he handed to me and put them back in the deed box, then closed the lid firmly and locked it, putting the gold chain around my neck before going back to my chair. "Mr. Holcroft—"

"Well?"

"I didn't know—nobody ever told me I had a Grandfather. I thought I had nobody of my own now. Do you think I'll be able to meet him?"

He hesitated, then said quietly:

"I'm afraid not. He is dead, these five months."

"Dead! Oh, no! Not him as well!"

"Of course. Why else should Lacey have advertised for an heir? Nobody knew where Edward Morley was and by the will everything was left to him or his issue."

"Then?"

16

"You own the Manor and all the lands, if you can prove your identity. And your legitimacy."

I blushed and looked down, because I had always understood that gentlemen did not talk of such things before ladies.

"But how can I look after the Manor and lands?" I said, after a while.

"If you take my advice you'll sell up and go away and enjoy yourself."

I stared at him in surprise, because this was the last answer I had expected.

"Can I do that with a family inheritance?"

"It will be better for you if you do."

Although his words had been spoken without expression I was suddenly aware of a cold, creeping fear, as if a draught of icy air had reached me. Then I tried to shrug the feeling off.

For what should I be afraid of? He could only mean that by selling I would be relieved of all the responsibilities of running what must be a very big house, and its surrounding lands.

But even though commonsense told me I was being stupid, I had to ask the question which was in my mind.

17

"Do you mean—there might be some danger to me if I don't?"

He made an impatient gesture.

"You're talking like a penny novelette," he said curtly. "I think you'd be happier, that's all. Don't forget, nobody knew of your existence until now."

I clasped my hands tightly together in my lap to stop them from trembling.

"You mean there are others at Clifton Manor besides you?"

"Yes, though strictly speaking Clifton is not my home and I am not always there nowadays. Your grandfather's wife and her son, Philip, are in residence there."

I felt as if the sun had broken through dark clouds.

"Then I've some relations? I'm not alone in the world after all?"

"No, though it might be better if you were," he said, but so quietly that I could not be sure that I had heard aright; and before I could ask him to repeat it he went on brusquely, "What do you mean to do now?"

"I don't know." Suddenly that lost, lonely feeling swept over me again. "Mama's illness—having to come here—

we had very little money saved and now—"

I stopped, knowing hopelessly that I could not tell my worries to this man who looked at me so impersonally out of unsympathetic · eyes.

But there was no need to, as I very soon discovered.

"You mean you've no money?"

I nodded miserably.

"I see. Well, if you decide to stay here I can lend you enough to tide you over until your claim is proved. When that happens you will have money enough. You'll be very comfortably situated and well able to set up your own establishment."

"But I'll still be alone," I answered quietly.

"You'll be able to engage a companion —some decent body—to live with you."

"Cold comfort when I've got some relations of my own."

His lips tightened.

"They are not really related to you, Miss Morley. I'm a nearer connection than they are."

"You?" I asked in surprise.

"Yes. I am the son of Tobias's cousin, so you see I'm a kind of second cousin to you."

"Then you must be about Papa's age?"

He looked irritated by my naïve question which I was ashamed of as soon as I had uttered it.

"Not quite," he said stiffly. "I'm thirty-four. Not yet Methuselah."

"I'm sorry. I didn't mean to be rude. Who then is this Philip?"

"He's your grandfather's stepson and is now twenty-four years of age. His mother is your grandfather's second wife. So you see how wrong you are to claim any of us as a close relative."

Suddenly I was tired of this argument, tired of listening to Jason Holcroft, of wondering why he seemed so anxious to keep me away from Clifton Manor, to have me sell my inheritance without seeing it or meeting the people of whom he spoke so coldly.

There was something very strange about his insistence. Yet what possible motive could be behind his endeavour to persuade me to do as he desired? Unless it might be that he himself was anxious to buy the

Manor and its lands, to become a landed proprietor. Well, I assured myself, if that was his reason he would soon learn that I was not going to allow myself to be gulled into acceding to it.

I looked at him challengingly, my chin raised.

"I don't care about that. I want to go to Clifton Manor and meet them. And I want to see Mr. Lacey myself."

His eyes, hard and cold, held mine for a long moment with an expression in them that made me feel irrationally afraid once again.

"Very well. If that is what you want I will make arrangements for you to visit them when I get back."

"I want to go now," I interrupted. "As soon as I can."

"Now!" he repeated disbelievingly.

"Yes. Will you take me with you? After all, you must know my claim is good. You've seen the documents, you've met me. What else is there to wait for?"

He was silent for a long time, his brows drawn together in deep thought. Then he said at last:

"So be it. I've tried to give you the best

21

possible advice but I see it's no use. Maybe surprise is the best form of attack, after all. I have to return tomorrow. Can you be ready?"

"Yes, indeed I can."

"Then I'll come for you at ten o'clock. Don't keep me waiting. We've a long journey ahead of us and I want to arrive before nightfall." He got up and walked purposefully to the door. "Until tomorrow then, Miss Morley."

He had gone before I could rise from my chair, so instead I sat where I was, looking back over this strange interview. And in spite of a not unexpected feeling of disbelief, I felt a little less lost and lonely.

Because I now knew I had some kin of my own, even though Jason Holcroft had denied it. What he did not understand was that in my position even distant cousins and step relations were very welcome.

Philip Morley. I said the name aloud, thinking how well it sounded. Philip was quite my favourite name for a man, and surely that must be a good omen.

And I had a home, too, if I wanted it, instead of the series of lodgings Mama and I had occupied since Papa's death ten years

22

ago. If only this news had come earlier so that Mama had known about it. Perhaps then she would not have died of that dreadful wasting disease. How happy we might have been in our own home, Clifton Manor.

Because I had no doubts. I knew it was mine by right of inheritance even though I had never heard of my Grandfather or the story of my parents' marriage. And I knew that no matter what Jason Holcroft might say, I was not going to sell it if I could possibly avoid doing so.

Jason, I thought scornfully. Impossible name for an impossible man. And at that moment I heard his voice saying, "I'd advise you to keep away from Clifton Manor," and was aware again of that creeping coldness of sudden fear.

I tried to overcome it, for what possible harm could I suffer? None, of course, as he had had to admit. It was only too evident that it was this dark arrogant man himself who did not want me there and was trying to frighten me into doing what he desired.

I was glad when at that moment the landlady came in, consumed by curiosity.

I told her all she needed to know, refused her offer of help as politely as I could, and when she had gone, went into the bedroom to begin to pack.

That did not take me long, as we had so few possessions, but I found it very distressing and I was exhausted by the time I lay down in my bed.

But in spite of that, I slept only in brief snatches, wakening again and again to the sound of Jason Holcroft's voice saying "I would advise you to keep away from Clifton Manor," yet knowing that I had to go.

That I must take up this inheritance which had come to me so strangely, no matter what the consequences might be.

2

I WAS ready long before Jason Holcroft came next morning, sitting fully dressed with the basket trunk beside me, while the landlady hovered solicitously round.

"Are you sure you're doing the right thing, Miss Morley?" she asked for the third time, looking at me with a worried frown. "There's no need for you to go. You can stay here till you find a position, with or without money."

I smiled at her gratefully.

"I know that, Mrs. Corner, and I do thank you for your kindness. Only I must go. These people are my only relations and I want to meet them."

"Well, you know your own business best, I suppose. Just remember you're welcome to come back here any time you want to."

"Thank you," I answered, and was glad when at that moment I heard the firm knock on the door for which I had been

25

listening. For I had not told Mrs. Corner about my inheritance and did not intend to if I could avoid it. I had only said that Mama had written to a lawyer about me —which she already knew because she had posted the letter and received the one that came in reply. The letter from which had transpired the strange happenings of the past few hours.

When Jason Holcroft strode into the room with Mrs. Corner hovering discreetly behind him, I was glad, too, that I had dressed in my most modish clothes. I was wearing the bonnet and mantle which matched my dress, all made by Mama and me from an old-fashioned and voluminous gown that the housekeeper at Mama's last place had given to her.

"Here, Morley," she had said contemptuously. "Madam gave me this old gown belonging to her mother. As if I'd wear such an out-of-date thing. Dark green, too. Such a dreary colour. But maybe it will do for you."

Mama had accepted it eagerly and we had carefully unpicked its many yards of material. From it we had made a day dress for me, with a little stand-up collar round the neck and a fitted bodice fastened with tiny buttons. I have a very small waist and do not need to use a corset, and the dress billowed away from it and swept down to my ankles in a very satisfactory way.

There had been enough material left to make a three-quarter length mantle, and from the plush that had trimmed the bodice Mama had made me a very fetching bonnet which I now wore on my so red hair, its ribbons tied under my chin in a big bow.

So as he wished me a curt good morning and looked me over with a critical eye, I knew I was looking as well as I could, even though I was not in the mourning garb which no doubt he would think I ought to be wearing.

"You're ready? Good." He picked up the basket trunk. "Is this all you have? Then come along."

He stood aside to let me go out of the room, then went past me to open the front door. But I did not hurry out immediately. I was determined not to go without saying a proper farewell to Mrs. Corner, who had been so kind to Mama and me.

"Goodbye, my dear. God bless you,"

she said, and kissed me. "Remember what I said. Come back to me if you don't care for your relations. Not that it's very likely," she added in a loud whisper. "If he's anything to go by, that is. Such a fine handsome man, isn't he?"

I was so taken aback at her praise that I was out in the street and had been helped into the open carriage before I recovered from my surprise. Though I had the presence of mind to turn and wave to Mrs. Corner as the two horses broke into a trot.

Covertly I looked at my companion, wondering still at the landlady's praise of him, seeing the thick, black brows and side whiskers, the mobile lips pressed together, the straight nose, the well shaped hands holding the reins so effortlessly. But in spite of all that, I could not agree with her. Because I do not admire dark men. My ideal would have fair curly hair and a bright open face. Apollo not Vulcan.

He glanced at me as if he was aware of my scrutiny, and I looked away quickly. It would never do to allow this proud and arrogant man to think I was in the least bit interested in him.

When we reached the edge of the village

I said a sad farewell to it in my heart, because I had come to it with such high hopes of health for Mama.

Then the speed of the horses quickened and the carriage began to sway alarmingly, so that I had to grab the rail at the side.

"Don't be afraid," he said calmly. "I won't overturn you, but we've a long way to go today."

"I'm not afraid. I was taken by surprise, that's all," I replied, but it was not true.

For a moment I, who had never before ridden in a carriage behind a pair of horses, had been very frightened indeed. But I had no intention of letting Jason Holcroft know that.

Any more than I was going to let him suspect how terrifed I was because I was going to a strange place to meet these people whom I had never heard of before yesterday.

As if he had read my thoughts he asked:

"Had your parents never told you about the Morleys, or Clifton Manor?"

"No. I was only nine years old when Papa died and afterwards Mama had to work very hard to keep me at school and look after us both. Sometimes when she was very worried she would say 'Ah, well, I suppose we've got our just deserts, your Papa and me', but she would never tell me what she meant. Do you know, Mr. Holcroft?"

"Yes. Tobias Morley arranged a wealthy marriage for his only child but he would have nothing to do with it. He was in love with somebody else, you see."

I heard the derogatory note very clearly in his voice and said sharply:

"Don't you believe in true love?"

"Oh, yes, when one can afford it. In this case, when Edward, your father, ran away with the housemaid, the price he paid was too great."

"You mean—my mother was the housemaid?" I asked, slowly.

"Yes. She was a charity child from an orphanage. Nobody knew who her parents had been. Because of it, Tobias Morley cast his son off. Disinherited him, or so we all thought."

I frowned, thinking of Mama and Papa and feeling glad that they had thought the world well lost for love, even though it had brought with it poverty and struggle. But I could remember how happy we had all been when we were together, in spite of everything. How much love and laughter there had been in our poor home.

I had never been aware of anything lacking in my life then, when we were all together. Only now, when I was quite grown up, was I beginning to understand to some extent that perhaps to enjoy such a sheltered life within one's family, no matter how happy, might not be the best training for living eventually in the world outside.

"You mean that in the end Grandfather didn't disinherit Papa?" I asked at last.

"Obviously not, though until he died everybody thought that he had made Philip his heir."

"Even though he was not of his own blood?"

"He was very fond of him, right from the first. Philip was only about seven years old when Tobias and his mother were married, and he gave him his name and brought him up as if he was his own son."

I was silent while I thought about that, then said quietly:

"Was he very distressed when he was told?"

"How should I know that?"

"I thought you might. I'm sorry I asked," I said stiffly.

"No doubt he'll give you the answer to that question when you see him."

"I expect he will." I intended to fall into a dignified silence after the snub he had administered to me, but I was too curious to find out about this man, Philip, who had caught my imagination so strongly to be quiet for long, and after a few minutes I said in a carefully casual tone, "You said he was younger than you. About twenty-four?"

"Yes," he replied briefly.

"But his mother would be quite old?"

"No. Dorothea was only twenty-six when Tobias married her."

"How old was grandfather then?"

"He was fifty-eight when he married and seventy-five when he died."

I made a quick calculation in my head and was appalled at the answer. Of course I knew that old men sometimes married very young wives, especially if they wanted an heir, but although I thought a husband should always be the elder, a difference of thirty-two years seemed very dreadful to me. Somehow sordid and desperately unromantic.

But then Mama had said again and again that I was too much of a dreamer and needed to come down to earth a bit, and perhaps she was right. Though in my heart I did not really think so. I could not bear to give up my dreams of romantic love so easily.

There were a lot more questions I would have liked to ask, but at that moment my companion pointed with his whip to the distant view and said:

"You can see the hills now. Clifton Manor is situated high up in them."

"Up there? But surely it must be very bleak and lonely?"

"Bleak enough in winter, and our neighbours are scattered. If you've been hoping for parties and enjoyment, you'll be very disappointed. There'll be little enough of that."

I coloured and said coldly:

"Of course I was not. You're forgetting, aren't you, that I am in mourning, and so are Philip and his mother, too."

He gave a sudden crack of laughter.

33

"Mourning? Why should they mourn for Tobias Morley?"

I was so incensed by his unfeeling answer that I was quite unable to reply, and we drove on in silence as I tried to make out what he had meant by that remark, though without avail.

We had begun a gradual climb into the foothills now, and I was becoming aware of a hollow feeling inside me, because I had eaten a very early breakfast and it was already long past my usual lunch time, when the pace began to slacken.

"We'll stop at the next inn for a meal and to change the horses," he said. "I left my own here on the way down. Stay in the carriage, please, until I've made sure everything is ready."

I did not answer, making up my mind to get out and stretch my weary limbs as soon as we reached the inn without reference to him, because I was quite tired of his autocratic ways.

What I had not realized was that I would be so stiff and chilled with sitting still for so long.

As soon as he stopped in the inn yard and jumped down, I also got up and started to scramble down. But before I knew what had happened, I had lost my footing and was lying on the ground, unable to move for the moment.

"What do you think you're doing?" his furious voice said. "I told you to stay in the carriage," and I was picked up and dumped unceremoniously on my feet.

I would have liked to appear dignified, even in my soiled mantle and with my bonnet tipped over one ear, and walk alone into the inn. Only unfortunately when I was upright I became quite dizzy and had to seize hold of his arm to steady myself, greatly to my annoyance.

"I'd better help you into the inn," he said in a long-suffering way, and taking my arm firmly in his, he almost ran me into the parlour.

I was thankful to sit down and partake of the meal and hot tea which were soon served to us, and gradually thawed out in front of the blazing fire. When I had eaten my fill and was feeling very much better, I said, formally:

"Thank you, Mr. Holcroft, for your kindness to me."

"I don't want your thanks. I'll go and

see the horses put to, if you're ready to move on. And for heaven's sake stop calling me Mr. Holcroft in that irritating way."

I am sure I must have looked as stupid as I felt, because he added impatiently:

"My name is Jason. As you're going to live at the Manor it would be as well to get used to calling me by it."

He was gone before I could reply, which was just as well as I did not know what to say. Never, I told myself, as I waited for him to come back, could I imagine myself on such terms of friendliness and intimacy with him.

He came in before very long.

"Ready? Then let's get away."

I followed him out into the yard and he helped me into the carriage, but instead of jumping in himself he looked at me frowningly.

"Haven't you anything warmer in your box? A fur tippet or a muff?"

I shook my head.

"No, but I shall be all right. I'm quite warm now."

"You won't be for long. Hold their

heads, Jeff," he said to the ostler, and ran back into the inn.

When he returned he was carrying two blankets and in spite of my protests he tucked one around my waist and legs and put the other around my shoulders.

"They should keep out some of the cold," he said and got into the carriage, taking the reins from the ostler, and we were off, bowling along at a great pace behind the two fresh horses.

The air seemed to have become much colder while we had been eating, and I was glad to huddle into the blankets he had provided for me. He himself seemed to be impervious to the cold. He sat, straight and tall beside me, his gloved hands holding the reins strongly, in complete control both of himself and the equipage.

I did not say much during the rest of our journey nor did Jason, as I would have to get used to calling him. I was beginning to feel very weary after the hours of unaccustomed travelling, as well as overcome by the hills which we were now among. They stretched on all sides, dark and in some strange way, menacing, deserted except for us.

To me, who had been used to flat land all my life, to places where there were always friendly people near at hand, these vast empty spaces, broken only by occasional small groups of trees, were intimidating. And I remembered again those strange words Jason had said.

Even in the parlour, with its warm glowing fire, they had chilled me. Now, circled by these lowering hills the thought of them filled me with a terror which caught at my throat, making it feel as if it would burst.

I wanted to tear open the top of my bodice which seemed to be constricting me and preventing me from breathing, and scream to Jason to stop. To plead with him to turn back because I did not dare to go on.

Only a total inability to say the words prevented me and then it was too late, because he turned to me and said quietly:

"That is Clifton Manor."

Those words, which might have been expected to increase my attack of nerves, instead had a calming effect on me. Possibly because the fact that we were now near enough to the Manor to actually see it, made me realize that I had come too far to retreat.

"There it is," Jason said impatiently again, pointing with his whip, and this time I looked along the line of it and had my first sight of my inheritance.

I peered through the gathering darkness and saw a big house, seemingly clinging to the side of a hill, very near the top, but it was still too far away for me to distinguish any particular characteristics.

I only knew that in its isolation, without another dwelling in sight and with the autumnal mists moving across it from time to time, it looked as sombre and menacing as the hills to which it clung so precariously.

"Are there no other houses near?" I asked at last.

"There are a couple of farms on the other side of the moors, but they are well beyond walking distance and in any case, they are occupied by tenant farmers with whom Tobias never had very much to do, and Thea and Philip nothing at all."

Those words seemed to complete my isolation and I shivered, suddenly feeling bitterly cold and even more fearful, seeing the mists that were slowly wreathing Clifton Manor as a cloak being put up to hide—what?

I did not know and could not even begin to guess. I only wished desperately that I had taken heed of what Jason had said and had not insisted on coming to that strange and frightening house, which looked as lonely as it seemed sinister.

But it was too late now. I straightened my shoulders and back, all my pride coming to the surface and telling me that I must not be a coward, but must face the future with fortitude and hope.

Because whatever might happen, for better or worse, the die was cast and I would have to make the best I could of it.

But in that moment I would have given up everything, inheritance, relations, Clifton Manor and the new knowledge of my parentage, to be back in Mrs. Corner's little parlour, safe and warm again.

3

IT seemed hours later, when I had almost ceased to know where I was or what I was doing there, I felt so cold and travel weary, that the pace of the horses slackened and I roused myself sufficiently to realize that we had turned off the road and were now following a track which wound steadily uphill.

"We're on Clifton land, now, Rachel," Jason said, breaking the silence which had existed between us for the last few miles.

"Are we?" I answered and clenched my hands tightly together, feeling a kind of excitement tingle through me in spite of my fatigue, and the fears which had beset me.

Because at last I was going to see and get to know the place where my father had lived all his life until he and Mama had left it to set forth into life together with nothing but great love and high hopes.

Though when we turned in between

stone pillars surmounted by an indeterminate animal holding a shield, through high iron gates standing hospitably open, it was already too dark to see Clifton Manor as more than an indistinct bulk still shrouded by wisps of white mist, without a light to be seen anywhere. Then we drove round the corner of that bulk into a yard bright with flaring lamps, and seeing them my spirits lifted and some of the tension which had been building up inside me all that day, left me.

The horses were reined in and a groom came running to hold their heads. Jason leaped down then almost lifted me from the carriage before going to the groom who was already unharnessing the horses.

I stood where he had left me, shivering a little in the cold wind, wondering what was in store for me at this place to which I had come so recklessly to cast my lot among people who might resent my very existence, and with reason if everything Jason had told me was true.

And although I found him both irritating and arrogant, and resented his calm assumption that I knew nothing and was unable to take care of myself, I had a strong desire to cling to him as the only link between my old life and the unknown new one.

The groom began to lead the horses away and Jason came striding over to me.

"Come along, Rachel. We'll go in through the kitchen entrance. Mrs. Ramsden is sure to be there," he said, and I went with him without a word as he set off at the brisk pace which seemed to be habitual to him.

We rounded the corner of the house and I saw that this side was well lighted, a mellow glow streaming out of the ground-floor windows on to what was obviously the kitchen yard. Jason pushed open a door and we were in a big kitchen, warm and redolent with the smell of baking and brightly lighted by a number of hanging oil lamps.

There was such a welcoming look about the place, and in the smile of the woman in a voluminous white apron who turned round from the range, that the rest of my fears receded into the background.

For what could possibly hurt me in that homely, bright kitchen?

"So you're back then, Mr. Jason," the woman said.

"Yes, and I've brought a visitor with me. This is Miss Rachel Morley, Mr. Edward's daughter. Mrs. Ramsden, Rachel, who takes such good care of us all."

"Away with your flattery," Mrs. Ramsden said, her face creasing into laughter lines, laughter which disappeared when she came closer to me, to be replaced by an expression which looked to me very like dismay.

Then she lifted her hands in astonishment and said:

"Lord bless me! There's no need to tell me who you are. Gave me a proper turn, so it did, seeing you standing there looking the spit and image of old master! I thought for a minute—but there. You don't want to hear about my stupid imaginings."

I smiled and held out my hand to her, relieved that the look of dismay had such a rational explanation and annoyed that I, who had never before indulged in such odd humours, should be so stupid.

It was all Jason Holcroft's fault, I told myself crossly, as I divested myself of my

44

mantle and bonnet as Mrs. Ramsden suggested. It was he who had first sown the seeds of doubt and distrust in my mind.

"Now sit down here and warm yourself while I make a brew of tea. You're fair chilled, I'll be bound, with that cold ride."

She bustled about, making the tea from water already boiling at the side of the fire, and setting out some of the cakes she had been baking on a plate.

"There you are, my dear. You'll feel better when you've taken something to eat. And you, too, Mr. Jason." Then she added quietly to him, "Mr. Philip's back."

"When did he arrive?" Jason asked sharply.

"This morning, late on. He's out now. I expect he's ridden over to visit Miss Ainsworth so I doubt if we'll see him this night."

I felt a wave of disappointment sweep over me at her words. I had been delighted to know that I might soon meet the man who had caught my imagination, but now it seemed as if I would have to wait a while longer before making his acquaintance. And, in addition, it appeared that he might

45

have some romantic attachment in the district. Because I had dreamed—Then I pushed that thought away from me, telling myself I was being silly as well as childish.

"And Mrs. Morley?" I heard Jason ask.

"She's in her room, as usual. Does she know about—?"

I saw the oblique glance she cast at me and wondered at the worry in her voice as she asked that question.

Jason shook his head.

"No. I thought it best to tell her myself. I shall go and see her as soon as I've tidied myself up. Will you look after Miss Rachel?"

"That I will. She'd better have the best spare room for tonight, I think."

"Just as you wish," he answered, and I was beginning to get annoyed because they were discussing me as if I was not there, when he came and stood beside me, looking down at me without a smile. "Mrs. Ramsden will look after you, Rachel. I'll see you later on."

He turned away on the words and left the kitchen. As he disappeared I had a strong desire to call after him, to beg him not to leave me alone in this strange house.

46

Luckily he was gone before I could give way to that impulse, which was just as well. I could imagine the contempt in his eyes at such an exhibition of cowardice.

Mrs. Ramsden lit a candle and took me up the back stairs, that apparently being the nearest way from the kitchen premises to the bedroom floor. We went through a baize-covered door on to a long passage, inadequately lighted by two hanging lamps which left the end of it in shadow, so that I could not see its whole length.

About a third of the way along, as near as I could judge, she opened a door and went through it before me, lighting the candles on the mantelpiece and dressing-table from the one she carried.

"We don't have any gas here, my dear," she said as she bent to light the fire which was already laid in the grate. "We're too far from the nearest town. So we have to make do with lamps and candles." She looked round critically, then lit an oil lamp standing on the table beside the bed. "That's better. Tomorrow we'll redd up master's old room for you and you can transfer to that, so don't do too much unpacking."

I looked around me, thinking how cosy the room looked, with the fire already burning up and reflected in the brass fire irons, and I said as much enthusiastically to the housekeeper.

"I'm glad," she said, obviously pleased by my praise. "I'll send Meg up with some hot water for you and she'll bring your box, too. Then later on she'll put a hot brick in your bed." She looked at me, shaking her head in amazement. "Eh, I've never seen anything like it, the way you favour old master."

When she had gone I sat down on the stool in front of the dressing-table. I had never been in such a beautiful room in my life. It was big and well-furnished, with candles in silver candelabra on the mantelpiece and dressing-table, and on the floor a thick carpet, which to me was the acmé of expensive comfort.

I twisted round on the stool and looked earnestly into the mirror, trying to make out what it was about me that had caused both Jason and Mrs. Ramsden to say how like I was to my Grandfather.

Certainly Mama had never mentioned it, even when I had complained as I did so often about my red hair. She had only said I ought to be glad to have such definite colouring and the kind of pale matt skin that went with it and which I never had to take care of as other girls did their complexions.

Of course I had been grateful about that, but I would have preferred my hair to be golden and my eyes to be my favourite blue, not the colour which more often than not seemed green and which my schoolfellows had jeered about.

"Cat's eyes," they had called them, and though I had never admitted it to them, in my own heart I had agreed.

Now as I gazed so earnestly at my mirrored face I was glad for the first time in my life because there seemed to be no doubt in anybody's mind that I was really a Morley.

I looked round as the bedroom door opened and a young girl came in wearing a print dress and a white cap and apron and carrying a steaming brass can.

"Here's your hot water, Miss," she said, bobbing a curtsy.

She put it down and went outside again

to bring in my basket trunk which she deposited at the end of the bed.

"I'll bring up a hot brick later on, Miss. Is there anything else you want? Can I help you to unpack? Or change your dress?"

"No, thank you—Meg, isn't it?" I said, not wanting her to see the few, poor clothes I had, or to know that the dark green dress I was wearing was the only really decent one I had. "I can manage, but I'd be glad if you'd come back and show me where the dining-room is."

"Yes, to be sure, Miss, though they allus gathers in the hall first. I'll come back in about half an hour, shall I?"

"Please, Meg. Thank you," I said.

I was quite ready when she returned. I had made a refreshing toilet, had shaken out and tidied my dress as well as I could, and had brushed my waist-length hair vigorously before pinning it in a chignon.

Then I had made sure that the key to the deed box was still safely on my gold chain before tucking it away inside my bodice as I had promised Mama I would.

"This way, Miss."

We turned left outside the bedroom and

Meg guided me down the main staircase, an elegant curving structure which led into a large hall, its perimeter in darkness where the golden lamplight did not reach.

There was a huge fire blazing in a stone fireplace which seemed to occupy the whole of one wall, and Jason Holcroft was standing by it, a glass in his hand.

I breathed a tiny sigh of relief when I saw him because he was still wearing the clothes in which he had travelled, just as I was.

It was not until later that I understood with surprise how thoughtful this was of him, when I discovered that normally everybody changed for the evening meal in this house.

He watched me walk down the stairs and when I reached the bottom said quietly:

"Is your room comfortable? Have you everything you need?"

"Yes, thank you." I smiled at Meg. "It was kind of you to bring me here."

She bobbed a curtsy.

"Shall I come back for you, Miss?"

"I'll see Miss Morley safely to her room, Meg," Jason cut in, and waited until she was out of sight on her way to the kitchen before adding: "Can I give you some wine?"

I hesitated, looking at the pale amber liquid in his glass, wondering what it tasted like. I knew I ought to refuse, but suddenly I felt quite reckless.

"Yes, please," I said, and watched as he poured out a modest half glass and handed it to me.

For a moment I was tempted to ask him to fill it up but caution intervened and I did not. And I was thankful I had not when I sipped it. It tasted vile and it was all I could do to stop myself from shuddering.

I saw his rare smile light up his face and knew he had read my thoughts, but before he could say anything there was a sound from the rear of the hall and a double door swung open.

Through it came a man bearing in his arms what appeared to be a bundle of clothes. As he came nearer I saw that he carried a lady who was wearing a very pretty gown of some filmy black material. She had bright golden hair which was dressed high and elegantly on her small head, with pretty curls escaping to frame her heart-shaped face.

She looked very young and fragile as he carefully laid her down on the sofa drawn up near to the fire, though when I came to look at her in a stronger light, I could see that she was not really as young as she had seemed at first sight.

"Well, Jason," she commanded, as soon as the man had gone, "introduce me."

"This is Mrs. Morley, Rachel," Jason said in his usual calm way. "Rachel Morley, Thea."

The big blue eyes looked at me speculatively and without any warmth.

"So you're Rachel Morley," she said, and I waited for her to exclaim as the housekeeper and Jason had done at my likeness to her husband, my Grandfather, but she did not. "Jason told me he had brought you here," she went on, "so I made an effort and came to meet you." She looked at Jason reproachfully. "It was a great shock to me. You ought to have prepared me first, instead of precipitating her into our midst like this."

I felt the hot colour rush into my face and knew a desire to apologize to this pretty elegant woman who was my Grandfather's widow and, looking at her, I could no longer wonder that he had fallen in love with her, even though, unexpectedly, she appeared to be an invalid.

"Rachel was left quite alone, Thea," Jason answered curtly, "and I thought it better to bring her here without delay and place her in your care as her stepgrandmama."

I saw the sudden brilliance of anger in her eyes, yet when she spoke her voice was as sweet and gentle as before.

"Knowing how poor my health is? That was not well done of you, was it?" She paused as if waiting for a reply but he did not oblige her and she went on plaintively, "Why are you dressed like that, Jason? Are you not dining with us?"

It was then that I discovered how very thoughtful he had been as he answered calmly:

"Rachel had nothing ready to change into, so I am keeping her company. I hear Philip is home."

I looked up eagerly, anxious to hear more about this man who had caught my interest, wishing I could see him, so I was pleased when she said:

"Yes. He has gone to call on dear Elaine but I am expecting him back soon. I sent Jim after him with a note telling him of Rachel's arrival."

Jason frowned.

"There was no need to take all that trouble."

"I thought there was. Philip will be anxious to greet his new cousin, just as I am pleased to do so."

"Thank you," I stammered, and was glad when Mrs. Ramsden came in at that moment to tell us dinner was ready.

"Shall I carry you in, Thea, or aren't you feeling strong enough to sit up to the table?" Jason asked.

She looked at him, her lips thinning into a straight line, though if she was really annoyed it did not sound in her voice. I was beginning to respect her for the strong control she had over her emotions.

"I shall be all right if you prop me up with cushions." Then when he picked her up as if she was no weight at all, she added with gentle pathos, "So rough, Jason."

But I noticed the way she curled her soft

white arm closely around his neck as he led the way to the dining-room.

I had expected to feel too shy and strange to be able to eat, but when I saw the food I realized how very hungry I was and did justice to the excellent meal Mrs. Ramsden had provided for us. Which was as well, because Jason and Dorothea—Thea as he called her—ate very little at all.

Nor did we speak very much, perhaps because either Mrs. Ramsden or Meg was with us most of the time. It was not until we were back in the hall which seemed to serve as a drawing-room that Thea said:

"Now, Jason, tell me all about this young lady who has come here to deprive my dearest Philip of his inheritance."

I was very taken aback by this direct attack which was quite unexpected, and would not have known what to answer. I think Jason was at a loss for words, too, so that the interruption which occurred at that moment was very welcome.

"What a thing to say, Thea!" a gay voice cried, and I turned towards the stair-case, watching the man who ran down it with complete disbelief.

For he was the epitome of everything I desired in a man. Tall and slender, with a handsome face, fair curling hair and laughing blue eyes, he was my dream hero come to life.

"Philip, my dear boy! Come here," Thea said, and held out her hand to him. But he ignored her and came straight to me, smiling down at me in a way that made my foolish heart beat faster.

"Thea knows well enough that I had no hope of an inheritance nor any desire for it," he said. "Far better for my new little cousin to have it so that we get to know her at last." He took my hands in his and gripped them tightly. "Welcome to Clifton Manor. Welcome home, Rachel."

"Thank you," I said shakily, filled with emotion because of the kind way he had welcomed me, as so far nobody else had done. And, if his mother was to be believed in spite of his denial, he had the least reason of them all to be kind to me.

"You go too fast, Philip," Thea said chidingly. "Rachel's claim has not yet been substantiated—"

"But it will be, Thea," he interrupted, and I was shocked to hear him address his mother so familiarly. "If Jason has brought her with him, we can be sure all's right. He's so reliable."

I looked at Jason, wondering if the way Philip had spoken of him would make him ashamed of the things he had hinted to me, but he only stretched out his long legs across the fireplace and said calmly:

"Your mother is quite right. Until Lacey sees the proofs and accepts them, nothing can be taken for granted."

"Oh, you are both too cautious! Are we to wait until Lacey is recovered from his illness before claiming Rachel as cousin? That will take far too long."

"No. I've arranged for Rachel to see him tomorrow," Jason replied coolly, and I started at his words.

"Tomorrow?" Philip frowned as if Jason's answer had annoyed him and I wondered why. Then when he spoke again I knew, and felt happiness glow within me like a warm flame. "Another journey after travelling so far today? You're being very thoughtless, Jason. Rachel must be worn out."

"She'll take no harm," came Jason's unfeeling reply, which I was sure was typical of him. "She's young and strong. Don't waste your sympathy on her, Philip."

"That I cannot believe! Surely there is no need for all this hurry. I am perfectly willing to accept Rachel at her face value." He took my hand in his again, with such a kindly look that I was almost overcome by emotion again and could hardly say the words I wanted to.

"You are so kind. But I can assure you I have the documents to prove my claim—"

"Safe, I trust, little cousin," he said quickly. "Because you don't know—even here—" And he glanced towards Jason, then away again, with what seemed to me an oddly accusing look.

"Quite safe. They're locked in my deed box and I keep the key always with me around my neck."

"Good. Then there's no need to exhaust yourself rushing off to see Lacey tomorrow. You must stay here with us so that we can get to know you better."

"I'd like that," I began, but Jason interrupted me with all his usual arrogance.

"It's not nearly as convenient for me, however. I have a business to run and must arrange these things to fit in with that. Anyway, I've already sent word that we'll be coming tomorrow. If you are so tired, Rachel, I suggest you retire now and have a good rest."

I felt a surge of irritation that prevented me from speaking, but I had a friend now fighting for me!

"Retire already," Philip protested. "I've hardly spoken with her! Don't leave us yet, little cousin. Come and sit beside me and tell me more about yourself."

I was absurdly pleased by his words but that sudden spurt of anger had been followed by a lassitude which made the thought of my bed and the quietness of my room after all the stress and strain of that day seem very desirable.

So that although I was loth to do as Jason suggested, I heard myself saying:

"Thank you, but it will be better if I retire now. I am feeling tired—"

"Poor Rachel," Philip said gently. "Then you must of course do so. Let me escort you to your room."

He moved towards the table at the foot of the staircase on which the night candles were placed, and lighted one of them.

As he did so, Jason got up and came across to me, saying in an urgent whisper:

"Rachel, take care! Watch out for—"

"What are you saying, Jason?" Thea interrupted languidly. "Let us all hear."

Philip turned round quickly and Jason said no more, but moved away from me and stood frowning across at us, his lips tightly compressed.

"Come along, Rachel," Philip said. "Which room has our dear Ramsden given you?"

"I believe it is the best spare room."

I murmured polite goodnights to Thea and Jason then joined Philip at the bottom of the stairs. He tucked my arm under his and we went upstairs together. When we reached the top I glanced back.

Jason was still standing where we had left him but he was watching us, the dark frown still on his face. While from the sofa Thea watched him, her expression hidden by one white hand shading her face.

Then, obedient to the pressure on my arm, I went with Philip along the passage to my room.

"Here we are."

He opened the door and went inside, lighting the candles which I had snuffed before going downstairs from the one he carried.

Then he smiled down at me.

"Goodnight, Rachel. You have your deed box safe ready for tomorrow?"

"Yes. It's hidden in my basket trunk."

"Good. You can't be too careful with it. Sleep well, little cousin."

He bent and brushed my cheek with his lips. When he had gone I stood where he had left me, looking at the closed door, my hand against the cheek he had kissed, lost in a happy dream.

I had been so afraid of coming to Clifton Manor and of meeting my new relations, but now I knew how foolish I had been. They could not have been more welcoming, or more kind. Especially Philip. Apollo, I thought happily. The Apollo I had been waiting for all my life.

Then I told myself sternly not to be silly. I had barely met Philip Morley, had hardly known him for one hour. It was quite ridiculous to be already daydreaming about him.

Yet when I finally got into bed, grateful for the warmth of the hot brick Meg had put there, he still filled my thoughts.

4

WHETHER it was the excitement of meeting a man who was the epitome of all my dreams, or because I was too emotionally tired, both physically and mentally, to rest, I do not know.

Whatever the reason, the fire which had been burning comfortingly when I got into bed had almost died down and I was still wakeful, even though the room was now in darkness.

There was no sound to be heard, except a soft whisper as the ash settled in the grate, and I turned over restlessly, determined that this time I would relax completely and allow sleep to take over.

I lay quietly, breathing evenly and deeply, letting my thoughts drift where they would, when I heard a sharp click and was instantly wide awake and taut as a bowstring again.

I raised my head, hardly breathing, and

saw a ribbon of light increasing as the door was slowly opened.

"Who's there! What do you want?" I said sharply, and immediately the light disappeared as the door was swiftly closed again.

I sat up, my heart beating quickly, fumbling for the matches on the table beside the bed, and struck one with trembling fingers. I lighted the lamp and looked around me, but there was nobody there.

I peered at the door which seemed to be closed, then forced myself to get out of bed and go and check it, carrying the lamp with me. It was tightly shut, yet I was sure I had not dreamed that widening ribbon of light.

I held my breath, listening intently, hardly aware of the cold air creeping around my bare feet, but the only sound I could hear was the thudding of my own heart.

I knew I had to open that door and look outside, but for a minute I could not summon up the courage. Then I pulled myself together. "Coward!" I whispered scornfully, and grasping the handle, I turned it and pulled the door wide open in one movement.

There was nobody there and after another moment of indecision I stepped outside, holding the lamp high before me, trying to see beyond the feeble light it cast, my ears stretched to hear any sound, but all was quiet.

I heaved a sigh of relief and was just about to go back into my room when I thought I saw something at the end of the passage, a deeper shadow among the shadows. Then there came a small sound, as if a door had closed quietly somewhere, and in a moment of blind panic I whisked back into my room and shut the door, leaning against it, my breast heaving as if I had been running for a long time.

Somebody had been there, I was sure now that I had not dreamed it. Yet who could it have been? I could hear Jason's voice whispering:

"Rachel, take care! Watch—"

Watch, he had said, but for what? What could harm me in this house? I did not know and my reason told me my fears were without foundation. Yet even while I admitted the truth of it, I knew I could not stay alone in that room for the remainder of the night without making sure it could not be entered again.

In the light from the lamp I could see the key in the lock and turned it, then tried the door to make sure it had caught. It had, and I felt a surge of relief shudder through me. I was safe now.

For the first time I realized that I was shivering with cold and reaction, and I got back into bed, pulling the clothes high around me, after turning down the lamp to cast a faint light which I found comforting.

I did not expect to sleep after the fright I had had, but I must have gone off almost at once, because the next thing I heard was a knock on the door and Meg's voice calling to me.

For a moment I did not know where I was, then I remembered and, still half asleep, got up and hurried across the room to open the door.

"Good morning, Miss. It's seven o'clock and I've brought you some hot water. Mrs. Ramsden says breakfast will be in the kitchen as soon as you're ready, if you don't mind."

She did not seem to find anything

strange in my locking the door, so I did not refer to it, either.

"Thank you, Meg. Will you come back for me in about quarter of an hour? I'm not sure I can find my way to the kitchen yet."

"Be sure I will, Miss." She put out a shy hand and touched the thick plait of hair hanging over my shoulder. "Eh, you've got lovely hair, so long and pretty. Shines like red gold in the sun, so it does."

Then with a quick bob she was gone, closing the door behind her.

I washed quickly and put on my green dress again, then hesitated, looking at my basket trunk and wondering what I should do. It did not lock and Philip had told me to take care of the deed box. Perhaps after my scare in the night—?

I bent down and opened it, taking out the box, then picking up my mantle and bonnet as well, I waited for Meg to come for me. Jason had intimated that my affairs were keeping him away from his business and I was determined I would not give him the opportunity of saying I had kept him waiting for one minute.

When Meg came I went with her to the

kitchen, only realizing when I entered that light, warm room how cold I was, inwardly as well as outwardly.

Jason was already there and he got up as I came in and pulled out a chair for me at the table.

I thanked him, responding mechanically to his greeting, and as I sat down Mrs. Ramsden put a plate of porridge in front of me.

"Now eat that, my dear. It'll help to keep you warm on the journey. There's nothing like a good breakfast to put heart into you."

I ate as much as I could of the food she served to me, not wanting to upset her, although I found it an effort to swallow. I could hear Jason and Mrs. Ramsden talking together but I did not take any part in their conversation because my own thoughts were occupying me too much.

I was trying to make up my mind what to do. Should I tell Jason what had happened during the night? I needed to talk about it to somebody, yet in the kitchen, surrounded by people who were being so kind to me, I found the memory barely credible. And if I felt like that, I would hardly be able to make Jason take my story seriously.

I sighed, knowing that I could not face the disbelief and contempt at my cowardice I would see in his eyes, and pushed my plate away from me.

He got up at once, saying:

"If you're ready, Rachel, I'll go and see the horses put to, then come back for you."

"I am ready now," I said, getting up also. "I have only to put on my bonnet and mantle."

"Good. Then come along with me to the stable yard." He stopped, looking frowningly down at me as he helped me on with my mantle. "Still in the same clothes? Could you find a couple of rugs, Mrs. Ramsden?"

"Surely, sir. There's plenty in the closet. I'll go and get them."

"You need not have troubled Mrs. Ramsden. My dress and mantle are quite thick, you know."

"Not thick enough to keep out the cold morning air. Don't be so prickly, Rachel. You must learn to accept things with a little more grace."

I flushed hotly and after a moment mumbled an abrupt apology.

"You'll have to buy some more clothes, more suitable to your present situation."

"I'm sorry my clothes don't suit you," I said with all the dignity I could muster, "but I cannot afford anything better."

"Don't worry about that. I will lend you the money until everything is cleared up."

"No thank you," I said, lifting my chin proudly. "I've never borrowed money in my life, and I've no intention of doing so now."

"Please yourself," he answered indifferently, and I thought with anger how impossible it was to penetrate the armour of pride and arrogance in which he was wrapped.

Mrs. Ramsden came in then with the rugs which was just as well, because I might have said more than was seemly. Jason took them from her with a word of thanks, then said to me:

"Come along, Rachel."

I picked up my deed box and went with him to the stable yard, where the horses were already harnessed to the carriage, with a groom in attendance.

He helped me up into it, then wrapped the rugs around me as he had done once before, only these were not coarse blankets but were made of fur, soft and luxurious to the touch.

Jason climbed into the carriage beside me and took the reins from the groom, then we were off, trotting down the path towards the road in darkness which was just beginning to lighten gradually.

I looked back, but Clifton Manor was still as dark and mysterious looking as it had been the day before, and I faced the direction in which we were going again, wondering what was in store for me when this drive was over.

The air was bitterly cold and before long I was glad of the rugs Jason had provided for me, though I did not say so. In fact I did not speak to him at all. I could not forget his autocratic behaviour, even though he had been kind enough to think of my comfort. Until it occurred to me that it might be more of a punishment to make him talk rather than allow him to be silent. In any case, there were questions I wanted to ask.

"Where are we going?" I said abruptly.

He started, as if he had forgotten I was there, which was probably quite likely.

"To see Mr. Lacey."

"I know that, but where?"

"To his office."

"Will he be there? I thought he was ill."

"He has an office at his home as well as in the town. He knows we are coming and I am hoping he will be able to see us, if only for a short time."

"You mean you've brought me on what may be a wasted journey? Philip was right! You're very selfish, Jason Holcroft. Why couldn't we wait until the poor man is really better?"

"Because I want your papers in his hands as quickly as possible. Don't you?"

"Of course, though I can't see what difference a few days will make."

"The sooner the better, Rachel. These things take time to settle and until they are, you're in an anomalous position. You will need money, too, and will have to rely on Mr. Lacey to advance you some, as you won't allow me to."

I shrugged off-handedly.

"I shall want little while I'm in mourning."

"But you're not and whatever ideas your parents had, it won't do for you to be putting people's backs up by not conforming. You must get some proper mourning clothes, Rachel."

I knew he was right because I had already seen a questioning look in Mrs. Ramsden's eyes and in Thea's, but I was not going to let him know that.

"I don't care what other people think."

"But I do, for you. I'll ask Mr. Lacey to make you an advance, then I'll bring some cloth from my mill for you to choose from."

"You make cloth at your mill?"

"Yes, indeed. It is a very flourishing concern, well known in most parts of the world."

"Then you weren't dependent on Grandfather?"

"Of course not. The mill was my father's and his father's before him. Tobias helped me to run it when I was inexperienced, and in return I helped him to run the Clifton estate as he became older. But of course things will be different now."

I looked at him in dismay.

"You mean you'll leave me to do it all?"

I asked, appalled at the responsibility I had so light-heartedly undertaken.

"Only if you want me to. Otherwise I'll go on overseeing things for as long as you wish."

"Thank you," I said, relieved. "And Philip? What does he do? Does he work on the estate?"

"No. He lives mostly in London. He is training to become a lawyer."

"Like Mr. Lacey?"

"Perhaps. Who knows?" he asked and clamped his lips together on the words.

I said no more, having too much to think about then. So Jason, although he was not living at Clifton Manor any more, had been entrusted with the management of the estate by Grandfather. While Philip had been sent off to London to become a lawyer.

Yet Philip had been a favourite of Grandfather, had expected to become the heir. That did not seem to follow at all, because surely the future heir should have been taught all about the running of the estate and the farm?

I would have liked to ask Jason why this had not happened, but the set of his mouth after he had answered my last question prevented me. I did not think I would get any more information from him, no matter how I probed.

We had been descending fairly steadily for some time and away in the distance I could see a heavy pall of smoke which no doubt signified a town of some size. Nearer to us, down in the broad valley, were the chimneys of a big house, set within trees, and Jason said briefly:

"That is Lacey's house."

I looked at it with interest, thinking it was quite near, but more than an hour elapsed before we turned in between two high gates and stopped in front of a pretty, half-timbered house.

"Stay where you are," Jason commanded, and jumped down from the carriage.

I did as he said, watching him mount the steps to the front door, which was opened before he reached it by a manservant.

"Good-morning, Mr. Jason. Come in, sir. Master's expecting you."

"How is he, Henry? Well enough to see us?"

76

"He says he is, and he seems a good deal better. You'll not mind going up to his bedroom?"

"No. I'll bring Miss Morley in."

"I'll see to the horses, sir," the man called after him as he ran down the steps.

"Very well. Come along, Rachel."

He helped me down and we went into the hall, waiting there while the man went upstairs to announce us. He was gone some time and Jason paced the floor impatiently, while I sat quietly in a chair, my box on my knee, trying to hide my anxiety about the outcome of this visit, even though I knew my claim was a legitimate one.

When the servant came back he took us upstairs to where Mr. Lacey was waiting for us, sitting in a high-backed chair wearing a beautiful smoking jacket and cap, with a fur rug tucked around his knees.

"Come in, Jason," he said when he saw us. "And the young lady, too." He smiled at me, his old eyes keen. "So you're Rachel Morley?"

"Yes, sir."

"I was sorry to hear of your mother's

death, my dear, and sorry, too, that my wretched health prevented my coming to see you myself. But I've no doubt you found Jason a very satisfactory substitute."

"Thank you, sir." I held out the deed box to him. "All the documents are in here."

He took it from me and put it on the table beside him, and I pulled the gold chain over my head and gave him the key.

"Sit down, please. I suppose you've already been told how like your father you are?"

"Yes. Did you know Papa, sir?" I said eagerly, because so far I had met nobody who had done so.

"From his birth." He shook his head sadly. "He was a good loyal son and should never have been turned off. Well, now they are together and we will hope all their differences are resolved. Now, let me look at these documents."

He unlocked the box and took the papers out, examining them very carefully before looking at me again.

"Your parents were happy together?"

"Oh, yes, sir, very happy until Papa died. Then there was only Mama and me but we were still happy, even though we were very poor." My throat constricted with tears but I fought them back, determined not to give way in front of Jason Holcroft. "The locket," I went on with difficulty. "It holds their likenesses."

He opened it and looked at them for a long time, then he smiled at me and said quietly:

"We must be thankful your Grandfather didn't change his will before he died, as he always said he would, right from the day your father went away. But saying is not enough in law, even though certain people would like to make us believe it is."

"Mrs. Morley said Philip expected to be the heir. Couldn't something be done?" I asked anxiously.

"Perhaps if Mrs. Morley and her son were to set up their own establishment—"

"Oh, no," I interrupted. "I wouldn't like that. They're the only relations I have."

"Then, my dear, I would advise you to leave things as they are until everything is settled. You agree, Jason?"

"Yes," he said in his usual curt way.

"Pass me my tablets, Jason, and I'll give

Miss Morley a receipt for these. Then when my Chief Clerk comes later today we can start the legal formalities which are necessary to give this young lady her inheritance."

I looked at Jason, willing him to remember that I needed some money, but I need not have worried. He had not forgotten. As I was quickly discovering, whatever his faults, he appeared never to forget a promise, once he had made it.

"Rachel's savings were swallowed up by her mother's last illness," he said. "She will need a little money."

"I thought of that and I have it here for her." He put his hand into an inside pocket and drew out a roll of notes. "Now, perhaps you in your turn will sign a receipt, my dear."

I did so and took the money, holding it in my hands and thinking I had never had so much in my life.

"Please ring the bell, Jason," Mr. Lacey said, and after a few minutes the servant came in. "Is the coffee ready, Henry?"

"Yes, sir. I've put it in the drawing-room."

"Good. Then I'll say goodbye to you,

my dear. Go down with Henry. There are still one or two things I'd like to talk over with Jason, but he will soon follow you."

I rose from my chair and said goodbye to the kindly old man. The servant took me downstairs and left me in the drawing-room, beside the coffee tray in front of a blazing fire.

I did not pour out at once but sat looking at the roll of notes before counting them carefully. I had signed for fifty pounds, a fortune, and I had to make sure I had them all. I was rich!

I relaxed in my chair, looking back over the events of the past two days. So much had happened, my life had changed so dramatically, that it did not seem possible that such a short time had elapsed. Yet it was true.

I considered, too, the question I had heard Mr. Lacey ask as I went out of the room upstairs.

"Is everything all right, Jason? There was no trouble?" he had said, and I could not imagine what he had meant.

Though of course he was probably not talking about my affairs at all. He and Jason would probably have more important matters to discuss, perhaps connected with the mill.

It was not long before Jason came in and I poured out the coffee, handling the heavy silver in a way which pleased me.

"Thank you." He took the cup from me and sat down at the other side of the fireplace.

"Is everything all right?"

"Yes, subject to some more information which must be obtained. But the clerk will see to that."

"What is the matter with Mr. Lacey?"

"He has a weak heart, which means he must take great care. How much did he give you?"

"Fifty pounds!" I said in an awed voice. "That is far too much for clothes."

He smiled.

"I don't think it will go quite as far as you expect, Rachel."

"But I mean to make everything myself. Mama and I made all our clothes. I was apprenticed as a seamstress, you know."

"Were you?"

"Yes. Of course, I didn't do any cutting out. I'm not sure how I'll go on there, but no doubt I'll manage."

"Would you consider employing my mother's former sewing woman? She is very reliable, even though she is getting old."

I hesitated.

"Would she be very expensive?"

"No. And you will probably have a lot of business matters to see to, and will need help with your dressmaking."

"Then perhaps I had better employ her."

"Good. I'll bring her to you. She is a very good dressmaker." He hesitated, then said casually, "Have you ever ridden a horse, Rachel?"

"Yes, though not like a lady." I laughed. "Once we lived in the country, when I was about twelve years old. Mama worked on a farm where they bred horses. I used to ride them, bareback, when I got the chance. I don't know if I could do it now."

"You won't have forgotten. I'll find a suitable mount for you then you won't be tied so strictly to the Manor grounds. You will have to have a riding habit made, as well."

"I mustn't spend all the money on clothes! I shall need it for other things."

"What things? As long as you keep a few pounds for odds and ends when the gypsies call—"

"Gypsies? They come to the Manor?"

"Yes, selling combs and ribbons and laces. Sometimes stockings, too, though it's as well not to enquire too closely where they got them from."

"And it's all right to buy from them?" I asked anxiously.

"Yes, most of the ladies do, especially when they are a long way from town as you are."

I was silent, lost in a blissful dream, until Jason said at last:

"We must go, Rachel. Shall I take charge of your money?"

I hesitated, but only for a moment, because I had nowhere properly to keep such a large sum.

"I'd be glad if you would, and thank you for being so kind to me."

"That isn't difficult," he said abruptly, and walked over to the door and opened it for me to go through.

The manservant saw us off the premises,

his fingers closing over something Jason had pressed into his hand. But I had no interest in anything like that.

I could only think of the new clothes I would be able to buy with the money Jason was holding for me, and of the horse I was going to ride. Ever since those carefree days on the farm I had longed to ride again, and now this man, who was such a strange mixture of arrogance and kindliness, was going to make it possible for me.

I seemed to be getting more and more involved with him, falling deeper and deeper into his debt. Yet I did not see how I could help it when as yet there was nobody else to whom I might turn for aid.

Perhaps one day Philip might take his place.

I snatched my errant thoughts back from that direction. Why should he bother about me, with my pale face and red hair, especially when he already visited with somebody else, the lady he had come specially from London to see.

She must be very lovely, I thought wistfully. She would be elegantly and expensively dressed and probably rode magnificently.

I sighed without realizing I had done so. Philip was not for me, I knew, yet that need not prevent me from admiring him at a distance. And perhaps when Jason found a horse for me, Philip might sometimes ride out with me, when he had nothing better to do.

And my mind went off at a blissful tangent, picturing us riding together, me in my new riding habit which I was determined should be made in the very latest fashion.

Although I am afraid that the girl galloping at Philip's side who was supposed to be me, bore very little resemblance to the reflection I saw in my mirror each day.

5

IT was early afternoon when we reached the Manor, and I left Jason in the stable yard and went into the house by the kitchen entrance, which was still the way I knew best.

"So you're back, Miss Rachel," Mrs. Ramsden greeted me. "I suppose Mr. Jason's gone off without waiting for anything to eat?"

"Yes, he has. He said he had no time to waste."

"He'll kill himself one of these days, so he will," she grumbled. "Ever since old Master went, he's driven himself without proper rest, as if he isn't human like the rest of us."

I almost said I did not think he was, but prevented myself in time. I was beginning at last to guard my unruly tongue, as Mama had always implored me to.

"Mr. Philip's waiting lunch for you, so as soon as you're ready, I'll send it through, Miss."

"He shouldn't have done that!" I cried, horrified at the idea. "Please serve right away, Mrs. Ramsden. I won't be more than five minutes."

I hurried up the back stairs to my bedroom, taking off my mantle and bonnet on the way, and quickly tidied my hair and washed perfunctorily.

When I ran down the stairs to the main hall, Philip came to meet me, his hands held out and his handsome face smiling.

"Here you are at last! I was beginning to think Lacey had kidnapped you. How did you get on?"

"Quite well. Mr. Lacey's taken charge of my papers and is going to see to them. He gave me a receipt and—"

"Did he? I hope you have it safely."

I paused, trying to remember what I had done with it, but to no avail.

"I haven't got it at all. I expect Jason will have picked it up. I'll ask him tonight."

He frowned.

"Is he coming back here?"

I looked at him in surprise.

"Yes. This is his home, isn't it?"

"No, it is not. He lives in a house beside

his mill. He has a couple of rooms here where he keeps a change of clothes, but he doesn't live here. Or at least he didn't until Father died."

I was silent, adjusting to this information and wondering why neither Jason nor Mrs. Ramsden had told me about it.

"Now you're mistress of Clifton Manor, you'll have to tell him to go home," Philip said gaily.

"I can't do that! Anyway, Mr. Lacey says I can't change anything here until all the legal formalities are completed. I expect he'll go when he's ready." But strangely enough, that thought worried me not a little.

Because even though I found him irritating and autocratic, I had come to rely on him a great deal, and could not imagine how I should go on if he was not there to help me.

Meg came in at that moment to say lunch was served, and we did not speak again until she had left us to bring in the second course. Then Philip said suddenly:

"Rachel, I think you should get that receipt into your own hands."

"Why? It will be quite safe with Jason."

"Perhaps, but it is the only proof you have of your parentage and your identity." He spoke with strange emphasis in a way which worried me. "The receipt should be in your possession and yours alone."

"I'll ask Jason for it if you think I should, but I trust him to take care of it—"

"I hope you will always feel able to trust him," he said quietly.

Meg brought in our second course then and we talked of indifferent matters while she was with us. Though I did not forget what Philip had said and meant to ask him about it as soon as I could. Only no opportunity arose, because he wanted to know all about me and my parents.

"You've had a hard life, little cousin," he said at last, "but everything is going to be wonderful for you in the future. I will see to that."

"Thank you," I stammered, feeling the colour rush into my face. "You're so very kind. But everybody has been kind to me. Jason asked Mr. Lacey for some money for me and has promised to find a horse for me to ride—"

"Ride!" He got up quickly. "Do not, Rachel. It is dangerous in this place."

I stared at him disbelievingly.

"Dangerous? I don't understand you."

"I'm sorry. Of course you don't. It's just that—there have been too many accidents with horses here."

"Accidents?" I was bewildered by his words and showed it plainly.

"Then you don't know? Jason didn't tell you?"

"Tell me what?"

"That Thea, my mother, received the injuries which crippled her in a riding accident, and that Father was killed in one." His hands clenched into fists and he turned away from me. "Do you wonder that the very thought of you riding fills me with fear?"

"But why should it? Surely they were accidents—"

He whirled round.

"Accidents! Thea had been riding from a child. She was a wonderful horsewoman. Why should she suddenly be thrown from Revel? He and she were as one. And Father also, at almost the same place. No,

I will never believe they were accidents, never!"

"They both happened in the same place?"

"Yes, though Father was unluckier than Thea—if it is luckier to be crippled for life as she has been. Father was flung into one of the old pits and killed. His injuries—" He shuddered and covered his eyes. "Did nobody tell you?"

"No," I whispered, longing to take him in my arms, to hold his head against me and smooth away the pain and grief so evident in his posture.

"He couldn't! That doesn't surprise me," he said bitterly.

"What do you mean?"

I was frightened by his vehemence and he straightened up at once and came to me, holding out both hands.

"I'm frightening you, Rachel. I didn't mean to. Take no notice of me. Of course you must ride, otherwise you'll never be able to get away from here. Only you must let me go with you sometimes."

I was relieved by his words, some of my fear slipping away.

"Of course I will. I'd like you to come with me, more than anyone."

He laughed, slipping his arm around my shoulders and giving me a hug.

"Thank you, Rachel. I'll remember that. Now get your bonnet and mantle and I'll show you round the house and grounds." I started to move away from him to do as he said, but he pulled me back. "Don't let anything happen to you, will you? You're beginning to become rather precious to me."

"No, no, I will not," I stammered, so carried away by his final words that it was not until much later, long after he had left me, that I remembered what had preceded them.

"Don't let anything happen to you," he had said, and by then I had known a fear greater than anything I had felt in Mrs. Corner's parlour or as I held my lamp high in front of me and saw that dark shadow and heard the quiet sound of a door closing.

But at that moment I was only eager to look over the house with Philip, and he waited outside my room while I collected my bonnet and mantle. He took them off me, then led the way up the next flight of stairs, which were still elegant though not as wide as the main staircase.

"The staff rooms are through that door," he said, "and these are all guest rooms along here, with the exception of these at the end of the passage. Thea used to have those before her accident, but now she occupies two on the ground floor. It is easier that way."

He looked so sad that I did not press him to open some of the doors so that I could see what the rooms were like, but went downstairs again to the passage on which my own room was situated. He turned as if to go down to the hall again, but I stopped and asked the question which had been in my mind since last night.

"Who occupies the room at the end of this passage, Philip?"

"Down there? Those are Jason's private apartments."

"Jason's!" I echoed, and remembered that vague shadow I had seen and the sound of the door closing. Both had come from that end of the passage and surely therefore could only mean one thing. It was Jason who had opened my bedroom door during the night, then stolen away when he realized I was awake. But why should he do that?

"I don't wonder you fnd it strange that he should be given some of the best rooms in the house, while Thea was relegated to the second floor, but Jason lived here before we did."

"I see," I replied, though to myself I admitted that this aspect of the situation had not occurred to me at all.

"Jason is ten years older than me, and seemed quite grown up. His mother died when he was born and his father when he was twelve. Father was a second cousin only, but he took him in and gave him a home."

"But he doesn't live here now?"

"No, though he still keeps his rooms. When he left his boarding school Father found him lodgings with the manager of the mill, and he stayed there most of the time. So you see we didn't have much opportunity to get to know each other well. Perhaps that's why—"

I waited for him to finish that sentence and when he did not, said:

"That isn't surprising really, because you would be away at school, too, and—"

"No," he interrupted. "I didn't go to boarding school. Thea did not want it so I had a tutor. Father couldn't understand why, but I knew. You see, I was all Thea had left when my own father died, and she was afraid she might lose me, too."

I put my hand impulsively on his arm. "Grandfather couldn't blame you for that."

"But he did," he said ruefully. "I think that might be why—but we mustn't talk about that. I have said I don't mind him not making a new will as he promised, especially as it brought you to us, and you will think me a lying fellow if I start bemoaning it now."

He looked at me so drolly that I had to laugh.

"How could I think that of you. But I am sure Grandfather would never have been so unkind."

"Not of himself perhaps, but I am afraid Jason was never my friend and Father always listened to him. You know I am training to be a lawyer?"

"Yes. Jason told me."

"He would. At first Father was very keen on my taking up that profession. It was only later, after Jason had talked to him, that he was against it."

"You mean, Jason alienated Grandfather from you deliberately?"

"Yes. I am sorry to have to say this, Rachel, but there is very little doubt. If only I had been as wise then as I am now, things might have been different."

I frowned.

"In what way?"

"I realize now how wrong I was. How much happier I would have been learning how to run the farm and the estate. But Father was killed before I could tell him of my ambition."

He sighed heavily, and I said:

"But surely that makes no difference. You can begin to learn now."

He laughed without humour.

"Not if Jason can help it! He is making sure nobody has control except himself. If only he would be content with the mill and leave us Morleys to manage our own affairs. But he will never do that." Then his mood changed and he said with more gaiety: "But you don't want to hear about my troubles! Come along and see the rest of your inheritance, dear Rachel."

I put my hand in his arm and went downstairs with him, doubly sure that he was the best and finest man I had ever known; and already making plans to ensure that he did not suffer because Grandfather had made no provision for him in his will.

I determined to write to Mr. Lacey and ask him what could be done to put things right but, in the meantime, it was felicity just to be with Philip, tall and fair beside me, and I made the most of it.

The house itself had been extensively modernized over the years, with the exception of the hall which still had the original panelling and ceiling. I had not examined it properly until that day, and I was delighted with it.

"Father would never have it touched," Philip said. "Mama would have liked it made more comfortable and modern but he wouldn't hear of it."

"I'm so glad!" I said. "It is just the kind of room I like. One can imagine all kinds of wonderful things happening here. It has atmosphere, Philip."

He laughed.

"You're so romantic, little cousin. Don't let Thea hear you talk like that. She prefers the luxuries of life to all the romance in the world, and who would blame her? We were used to living in a town and when she first came here to oil lamps and candles, she thought she had returned to the dark ages."

"Oh, but I love them! We had gas, too, when we lived in London but the lamps here are so much more beautiful and give such a splendid, golden light!"

He hugged me against him.

"Such a very determined romantic, Rachel! So I will show you something I am sure you will love and not be afraid of. Come over here."

He took me over to one of the walls, and pressed one of the embossed flowers on it.

"There!" he said triumphantly and I gasped as a section of the panelling slid back, leaving a small, cupboard-like space in view.

"A priest's hole!" I cried.

"Yes, but watch again." He stepped into the little room and I followed. I could not see what he did as he blocked my view, but a door at the rear slid open, showing an oblong of darkness. "This is the entrance to a passage which used to lead to a cave in the hill. It's blocked now, but I believe it was much used by smugglers formerly, when the Morleys were less law-abiding than they are now."

"Oh, I'm so glad there is something like this in the Manor, though I'm thankful it has been closed up."

"You only want your romance at second hand, that I can see. Just like Thea. She insisted on the passage being blocked. It gave her strong convulsions to think anyone might be able to come and go without check. Come, let us go outside and look at the gardens."

He helped me into my mantle and I put on my bonnet, but we were destined not to do that together. As Philip opened the door and we stepped outside there came a sound of galloping hooves and a horse and rider swept round the bend in the drive, and came to a dramatic stop directly in front of us.

Philip gave a shout of delighted recognition and ran down the steps to greet the lady sitting so elegantly on the big horse, her guinea-gold hair bright under a riding hat with a plume, her face alight with merriment.

"Elaine!" he cried. "How wonderful to see you."

"I called to ask you if you would like to come riding with me," she said in a sweet soft voice.

"Of course I will. Come round to the stables and one of the grooms will take care of your horse while I change."

He took hold of the bridle and began to lead the horse away, his face upturned to that golden girl, leaving me still at the top of the steps, quite forgotten. But I did not blame him.

I knew without being told that this was Miss Ainsworth, and she was so beautiful that my faint hopes at once died away. For how could I imagine that Philip might fall in love with me, when so much wealth and beauty was before him?

I waited until they turned the corner of the house, then walked down the steps and along the path, feeling solitary and unhappy. When I reached the bend I looked back, seeing the Manor for the first time in daylight.

It was an impressive looking house, seeming to be bigger than it really was. It had a portico with Grecian pillars and marble steps leading up to the main door, with four big windows at each side. Above the door was an oval window, deep-set in the thick stone of which the Manor was built, and above that again the first-floor windows, all symmetrically placed, like those below. Those on the second and third floors, however, were of differing shapes and sizes and were most haphazardly positioned, giving a fascinating and romantic appearance to the whole. And above them all was a crenellated ledge with a small round tower at each end.

I was staring at it, delighted by its appearance, when my attention was caught by a movement at one of the windows on the second floor. It was as if a curtain had been dropped into place, veiling the upright female figure which, as I looked, seemed to disappear. Yet Philip had said those rooms were unused since his mother's accident.

I shivered suddenly, as if a goose had

stepped over my grave, as the saying is, sure that somebody inimical to me had been looking out at me. Then I told myself not to be foolish. For who could have been there?

Not Mrs. Ramsden or one of the servants. They would have been readily recognizable by the white aprons, while this figure I had seen had worn dark clothes. There was only Thea in the house apart from them, and she was unable to stand upright.

Unless it was her dresser who had been with her for years and looked after her so well? I had never seen her so would not be likely to recognize her, and it would be natural for her to be inquisitive about the stranger who had come so unexpectedly to the Manor, as I would have been if the situations had been reversed.

So why should that strange foreboding have remained with me as I crossed the lawn towards a nearby group of trees in which I was glad to lose myself to escape from the unseen eyes which seemed to be boring malevolently into my back?

I followed the path through them to come out on to a stretch of lawn bounded by a low parapet from which could be seen a vista which, on a clear day, must have been well worth looking at. Today, however, the mist was low again and I could see little beyond the hedge which separated a kind of ha-ha from the more formal part of the garden.

I had only stood there a few minutes, trying to get my bearings, when I heard a sound behind me. I moved to turn round and see who was coming and, when I thought about it afterwards, knew that the slight movement had saved my life.

I saw something sweep upwards, then felt a heavy blow which ripped along the side of my head and fell on to my shoulder. I staggered under the impact and my foot caught the edge of the stone parapet. Then I was over, rolling down the slope into the ha-ha, unable to do anything to save myself.

6

I CAME to myself to find Jason bending over me, calling my name and chafing my hands.

"Rachel!" he said urgently as I opened my eyes, trying to get his face, which loomed over me like a giant's, into focus. "Thank heaven! When I saw you lying down here I thought—"

"What happened?"

I tried to raise my head and cried out with the pain of it.

"You're hurt! Lie still."

"It's my neck. When I move it—"

"Wait. I'll raise you."

He put his hands under my head and shoulders and very gently lifted me until I was resting against him.

"Where is the pain, Rachel?"

It seemed to me that I was aching all over, but after a moment I was able to isolate a more intense soreness at the side of my head and in my shoulder.

"Here and here," I said, and

then remembered. I clutched at him tightly.

"Jason, I was standing at the end of the tree walk. I heard a sound and started to turn round. Something struck me. I must have fallen over the parapet, then—I don't remember any more."

His fingers were gently exploring my head and I winced when they reached a spot at the back of it.

"You've got quite a bump there. You must have banged your head as you went over, I think, and knocked yourself out."

Again the gentle fingers explored the side of my head and my shoulder, making me wince and feel sick, but I managed not to cry out.

"Nothing broken, by a miracle. You're a brave girl, Rachel. Will it be too much for you if I lift you and carry you into the house?"

"No, I can walk, if you'll help me. Please, Jason. I'd rather."

"Very well," he said, in a rather stiff kind of way, and I wondered if my rejection of his offer had offended him. I hoped not, but could not help it if it had. Something within me was impelling me to make as little as I could of the attack on me.

He helped me to my feet and I clung to him as everything whirled dizzily around me, but after a few minutes that sensation passed and I began to walk slowly up a short flight of steps to the top of the ha-ha supported by Jason's arm.

It seemed to take hours to get back into the house. We went in through a side door which I had not seen before, which led by a passage into the hall. There Jason made me sit down on the sofa while he went through to the kitchen premises.

While he was gone I closed my eyes, trying to understand what had happened, to visualize those few moments before my fall, and gradually I became certain in my own mind that somebody had deliberately tried to injure me. But why?

When Jason came back with hot milk into which he had poured a generous measure of brandy, I tried to tell him my suspicions.

"You must be mistaken, Rachel," he said curtly. "The knock on your head has muddled you. Drink your milk. It will make you feel stronger, then I'll take you to your room and Mrs. Ramsden will look after you."

I was too upset and sick both in body and at heart to argue with him, and meekly obeyed. Either the hot milk or the spirits he had put into it did revive me, and after I had drunk it all I was able to climb the stairs with the help of his arm and the banister rail.

Mrs. Ramsden was already in my room with Meg, and as soon as they took charge of me, Jason left. I let him go because I did not want to talk about what had happened to me in front of them. Though I was determined to make him understand that there really had been an attack made on me; that I had not imagined the whole thing. And somehow, in my present confused state, it seemed to be very important that I should do so.

"Eh, dear!" Mrs. Ramsden said in horror, as she gently eased my dress off. "Look at that shoulder! You'll be black and blue before you're an hour older, that you will."

"My face?" I asked, suddenly remembering the glancing blow which had ripped down the side of my head before my shoulder had taken the full force.

"It seems all right. Your hair probably saved you from injury there, but I'll bathe it and put some arnica on, just in case."

Quickly and gently they ministered to me and before long I was in bed, sipping the potion the housekeeper had prepared for me.

"Now, stay where you are till morning, then we'll see how you feel and maybe send for the doctor to look at you."

"Don't leave me!" I said, suddenly deeply and irrationally afraid.

"Nay, don't you worry. Mr. Jason says Meg's to stay with you. See, she's sitting there by the fire. You go off to sleep, my love."

I smiled at her gratefully, already almost overcome by the spirits and the potion I had swallowed, and must have fallen asleep almost immediately.

When I awoke the room was softly lit by lamplight and Meg was asleep on a truckle bed which had been set up beside mine. I felt better, though when I gingerly moved my head and shoulders, they were still very stiff and sore.

But my head was quite clear and so was the memory of what had happened to me. There was no doubt at all in my mind that some unknown person had struck me down and that I had only been saved from a broken skull because I had moved at the crucial moment and so had received a glancing blow instead of the full force of the cudgel, or whatever it was that had been used.

Somebody had meant to kill me. For the first time I allowed that thought to come into my mind and faced it squarely. Yet why should they want to do that? And why, having bungled, did they not come down into the ha-ha to finish the job? Perhaps because Jason had come along before they could do so?

I was still trying to find the answers to the questions which plagued me when Meg awoke and got up quickly.

"Oh, Miss Rachel, what must you think of me? Sleeping like this instead of taking care of you."

I smiled at her.

"I think you and Mrs. Ramsden are wonderful, Meg. You've both been so kind to me."

"You're easy to be kind to, Miss." She peered at the clock on the mantelpiece. "It's almost seven. Would you like some breakfast?"

"Yes, please. Lots and lots of tea and some bread and butter."

"That means you're feeling better," she said, with satisfaction. "Will you mind if I go and get it for you?"

"Of course not, Meg. I hardly knew what I was saying yesterday. It *was* yesterday?"

"Yes. You slept like a babby all evening and for the whole night."

"Were you with me all the time?"

"No. Mrs. Ramsden took over while I had my supper, but I stayed with you the rest of the time."

"Thank you, Meg. I won't forget that," I said with real and heartfelt gratitude.

"Mr. Jason'd have had my life if I hadn't! I'll go and fetch your breakfast, then, and mind, you're not to get out of bed till Mrs. Ramsden's seen you."

"I won't."

I watched her go out of the room and close the door firmly behind her, feeling warmed and comforted by the kindness I

111

had been shown. And it was Jason who had insisted that somebody should stay with me all night, anticipating that I might be nervous after what had happened.

What a strange mixture he was. So arrogant and impatient on the surface, yet seemingly filled with kindly and thoughtful impulses which took one by surprise.

Mrs. Ramsden brought my breakfast in at that moment and stayed with me while I ate it, keeping up a gentle flow of small talk. Then she examined my head and shoulder and expressed herself satisfied.

Meg brought up some hot water and my bruises were bathed and more arnica put on. My shoulder was black and angry looking but Mrs. Ramsden seemed to think it all the better for that.

When I had been washed, she brushed my hair and plaited it and finally gave way to my insistence, saying I could get up for a while if I stayed quietly by the fire in my bedroom. She wrapped me warmly in a rug and tucked a soft shawl around my shoulders before going back to her duties.

She had hardly left me when there was a knock at the door and Jason came in, carrying some books which he put down on a small table. Then he stood looking at me, the familiar frown between his brows.

"How are you this morning? I did not expect to find you up."

"I'm feeling better though still stiff and sore. Mrs. Ramsden says I must stay in my room today."

"She is quite right. The rest will be beneficial. I've brought you some books to read to help to pass the time away. Have you remembered what happened to you?"

"Yes. I told you yesterday. Somebody meant to break my head for me but I moved in time. Don't you believe me?"

"It is immaterial whether I do or not. What is important is whether you've told this story to anybody else."

"No, I haven't. Does it matter so much?"

"I think it does. I think you would be wiser to say you tripped over the parapet edge, and make no reference to anything else."

"Why?" I asked bluntly.

He answered me with another question.

"Have you considered what you are saying?"

"What do you mean?"

"You're accusing somebody here of trying to kill you."

"No, I'm not!"

"Then what are you suggesting?"

I was unable to answer him because I did not know. I was only certain that my memory of what had happened was clear and vivid. Yet Jason was right. Who would do such a thing, and why? For what had they to gain?

Certainly Philip must be exonerated because he was with Miss Ainsworth; Thea was a cripple and could not walk, and it would be foolish to consider Mrs. Ramsden or the domestics. The idea was laughable.

The only person who had been near was Jason himself, for he had been kneeling beside me when I came to my senses. How had he come to that particular place so fortuitously? What had he been doing, how had he looked when I had first opened my eyes? I frowned in concentration trying to conjure up a picture of him, but without success.

Then I was ashamed of the direction in which my thoughts were leading me when he said:

"I must only be thankful that I came home early to bring you a selection of materials as I promised. I also called on Lizzie and arranged with her to come up today and see you about making some dresses. When you weren't in the house I looked for you in the garden and found you where I did. And a great fright you gave me, too."

"You didn't see anybody lurking about? Somebody who your presence frightened away?"

The familiar closed look came back into his face.

"I thought we'd agreed it was an accident?" he said coldly. "Shall I tell Lizzie to come back another day?"

"No, there's no need to do that." Then with an effort I added, "Thank you for the trouble you've taken."

"I'll ask Mrs. Ramsden to bring her to you when she comes. The cloth has been put in the sewing-room for the time being, but no doubt Lizzie will bring it through for you to choose what you require."

"I need so many things," I said with a sigh. "Have you spent all my money, Jason?"

"Not quite all. Why? Is there something special you would like?"

I shook my head.

"No. Perhaps one day—I've always hoped—but it would be a terrible extravagance."

He smiled at me.

"What would be? Come, tell me, Rachel."

I sighed.

"You will think me silly, I expect, but once I saw a girl no older than myself getting out of a carriage and she had a kind of white fur about her neck and a huge muff to match. You will laugh, Jason, but I *coveted* those furs!"

"No, I would not laugh and perhaps they were not so expensive as you imagine." He hesitated, then said quietly, "Don't let what happened yesterday frighten you too much, Rachel. You have some friends here, remember. Now I must go to the mill, but I will come again to see you this evening."

He left me on those words and I closed my eyes, looking back over our talk together, trying to understand this strange man, but without success. His character was too complex to be easily read.

I picked up the books he had so thoughtfully brought for me to read, but I did not have a chance to look at them, because Mrs. Ramsden came bustling in, followed by an elderly woman in a neat, dark dress and snow white cap and tucker.

"Here's Lizzie come to see what she can do for you, Miss Rachel. Are you feeling well enough to be bothered?"

"Yes, indeed! I would have to be very ill indeed not to be excited at the thought of all the new clothes Lizzie is going to make for me."

"I'll go and fetch the cloth Mr. Jason's brought home then. I reckon he thought he was providing for a whole seminary of young ladies, not just one."

"Can I help you, Mrs. Ramsden?"

"No, thanks, Lizzie. Meg'll do that. You stay here and show Miss Rachel the patterns you've brought."

"Bring a chair and sit beside me, Lizzie," I said. "How exciting it is! I can't wait to see the patterns and the cloth."

"I thought some day dresses and some

gowns suitable for dining in. And Mr. Jason says you'll need a riding habit."

"Yes. He's going to find me a suitable mount. Isn't that kind of him?"

"He's the kindest gentleman in the world. There's many a tale I could tell about what he's done for me and others."

I smiled, interested in what she said though I put her enthusiasm down to the prejudice of an old retainer. Yet even so I had to admit that he had proved a friend to me, though I did not know what his reasons might be.

I would have liked to delve further into it and find out what Jason had done for her and others, but Mrs. Ramsden and Meg came in laden with different kinds of cloth.

I gazed in astonishment as they tumbled their burdens on to the bed.

"Goodness! I'm never going to need all that!"

"It's only the half of it. There's linen and cambric and trimmings of all kinds."

"But the cost," I said in dismay, thinking my fifty pounds would not go very far if Jason expected me to use all this material.

"Don't you worry about that, Miss Rachel. We'll choose the materials we need and Mr. Jason'll take the rest back. I think two or three day dresses and a skirt and jacket will do for the time being. As well as the riding habit."

"Yes," I said weakly, quite dazed by the way in which things were happening.

"You're in mourning, I believe?"

"Yes, for my mother, though she didn't believe in blacks."

"I think you ought to wear it, just the same, Miss Rachel. People'll talk otherwise," Mrs. Ramsden said.

"I agree," Lizzie answered quietly. "Now, Miss Rachel, if you'll choose the materials you want—"

"And Meg and I must get on with our work. Come along, lass," the housekeeper said briskly and they left Lizzie and me together.

I chose the materials, helped by Lizzie who was very knowledgeable about them, including a lacy one for a supper gown.

"This will make up well, Miss. Do you want a low corsage?"

"No, a high one, Lizzie. With long sleeves."

"I know just the thing." She leafed through her patterns until she found what she wanted. "There. Do you like it?"

"Oh, yes."

I looked down at the picture, trying to visualize myself in those flowing draperies and wishing they could be made up in a colour instead of black, a colour which might appeal to Philip.

As if she had read my mind, Lizzie said: "You're wrong to despise black, Miss Rachel. With your colouring it will look very well on you, and you're young enough to wear a touch of white at the neck and wrists."

"I'm nineteen!"

"Still young enough for the white touches. Now, I'll take the cloth you've chosen and go up to the nurseries. Have you a gown I can use for measurements?"

"Yes. The green one in the press." I made to get up but she pushed me gently back.

"I'll get it." She went over to the press and lifted it out. "It's a good fit?"

"Oh, yes. Mama and I made it just before she became really ill—"

I stopped, my eyes filling with tears as

I remembered how happy we had been as we cut out and stitched with no thought in my mind that Mama would be gone from me in such a short time.

"Then I'll use this," Lizzie said quietly.

"I can sew quite well, Lizzie," I managed to say. "Will you let me help? It will give me something to do while I'm sitting here."

"Of course, Miss. I'll be glad of your help."

She went out, taking the materials we had chosen with her, and I sat back in my chair, lost in a happy dream. I was going to have some new clothes, more than I had ever had in my life before, and it would have been very strange if I had not felt excited by it, even under present circumstances. And I had to admit that it was all due to Jason Holcroft, on which thought I dropped into a sudden sleep of weakness.

I was awakened by the door opening and for a moment thought I was still asleep and dreaming as I saw Thea being carried in by one of the outside male servants.

"Put me on the bed," she instructed, "and pile the pillows behind my shoulders."

121

He did as she commanded, then went out, and I stared at her, so surprised at her coming to visit me that I was unable to utter a word.

"Good-day, Rachel. I hear you've had an accident so I felt I ought to come and see how you are. Is it true?"

"Yes," I said baldly.

"How did it happen?"

For a moment I was tempted to tell her my suspicions, then remembered what Jason had said to me and did not give way to that impulse.

"I was standing beside the low parapet at the top of the ha-ha and turned round quickly. I must have caught my foot against it and I rolled down the slope and hurt my shoulder."

"Was there nobody else there?"

"I didn't see anyone," I answered cautiously.

She was silent for quite a time, then said:

"And Jason found you?"

"Yes."

"How very opportune! Remarkably so, in fact, but then one expects that kind of thing from him."

"He came back early to bring me some cloth he had promised," I said, feeling a surge of anger at her words which surprised me, particularly as Thea was only expressing my own thoughts. But it seemed very different to hear them expressed in her sugar sweet voice somehow. "When he couldn't find me in the house he came to look for me."

"And went straight to the ha-ha? I still say it was most suspiciously opportune. Are these what he brought?" she added, pointing to the cloth which Lizzie had stacked tidily at the foot of the bed.

"Yes."

"All very expensive materials. I hope you'll be able to pay for them, otherwise you might be in trouble with our dear Jason."

Again I was impelled to defend him.

"Mr. Lacey gave me enough money to buy what I need."

"What a lucky girl you are, Rachel. If my husband had lived another few days you would have got nothing, and Jason would have had to give way to my son. That death was very opportune for him also."

I was so horrified by her words that I could say nothing at all in reply, because surely she was insinuating that Grandfather's death had been contrived, had been brought about by Jason, and every instinct prompted me to refute that accusation. But I could find no words, and while I stared at her, she said sweetly:

"Press the bell twice, Rachel, and Harry will come for me. I'm tired now and would like to go back to my own rooms."

We sat in silence until Harry came in and, lifting her up, carried her out of the room. When the door closed behind them, I pressed my hand over my eyes, realizing that the visit she had paid me had made my head begin to throb again.

Why had she really come? Certainly not out of any regard for me or my welfare, I was sure. All she had done was to make me feel guilty because I was taking from her son the inheritance they had expected, and sow seeds of doubt in my mind about Jason.

Well, she had not succeeded in the latter. Somehow I could not see him as a villain, causing Grandfather's death and trying to bring about mine. It was ludicrous, and I shook my aching head, sure that I must have misunderstood her.

Yet I was still confused and uneasy, certain only of one thing. That I neither liked nor trusted Philip's mother. Instead of being sorry for her because she was crippled and unable to move about and must therefore be harmless, I felt a shrinking from her as if from something evil.

I knew no reason for that, except there was something in her glance, in her sweet voice, which repelled me, and against which I knew I must fight if I ever attained my dearest wish that one day her son might fall in love with me and make me his wife.

7

MRS. RAMSDEN came to visit me shortly after Thea had gone and as soon as she saw me, insisted that I got back into bed, and I was feeling so done up that I did not protest.

She gave me a draught for my headache and bathed my bruises again, then left me and I knew no more until Meg brought me my tea.

I was feeling much better by then and after I had eaten and drunk what was on the tray, began to look forward to the evening. Because then surely Philip would come and see me when he heard from his mother that I was confined to my room.

When Meg came back for the tray I asked her to brush my hair and tidy it for me and this she did, seeming to take pleasure in doing so. Then she carefully wrapped a shawl around me and went back to the kitchen, after making up my fire, and I was ready and eager for Philip to come.

But alas that mood did not last for very long, as time passed and he did not come. Then all my doubts rushed back into my mind. Why should he bother about me? Probably he had spent the day with Miss Ainsworth and would dine at her home and who would blame him, when she was so rich and so lovely?

Again and again I reminded myself that he had told me I was beginning to become precious to him. Nevertheless I could not convince myself that it was true, nor shake off the depressed, bereft feeling which had attacked me; nor did I try to stop the tears which slid under my closed lids and ran down my cheeks.

It was at that moment of hopelessness that the knock came at the door and I raised my head from the pillows, disregarding the pain of my bruised shoulder and called eagerly:

"Come in!"

But it was Vulcan who entered, not Apollo, and I could not hold back my exclamation of disappointment.

"What is it, Rachel?" He came quickly over to the bed and frowned down at me.

"Are you worse? Perhaps we should have sent for the physician, after all."

"No, I'm all right. Just stiff and sore. I thought you were—"

My voice wavered and I stopped, ashamed that I had almost given away my longing to see Philip to this man. But I might have known I could not deceive him and he left me in no doubt that he knew exactly what I had been going to say.

"Were you hoping to see Philip? You'll be disappointed, I'm afraid. He never goes near a sick bed."

"But I'm not sick!"

"True," he said with all his usual lack of sympathy, "but he doesn't believe that. You'll have to wait until you're on your feet again before you will gain your wish."

I was so aggravated by his contemptuous words that I sat up with a jerk, hardly noticing the wrench of pain in my shoulder and body.

"You don't understand a sensitive person's feelings," I cried. "You're hard, Jason. Hard and stony hearted."

He smiled.

"Are you expecting me to believe that you do understand? Come now, Rachel, you mustn't deceive yourself like that. We're two of a kind, you and I."

"Why, you—How dare you say that!"

He leaned forward and took hold of a strand of my hair, letting its length run slowly through his fingers.

"Beautiful silky hair, Rachel, and a beautiful colour, too, but it gives you away. Nobody with this shade of hair can ever be anything but a termagant."

"What do you know about it?" I flashed back at him. "You hardly know me. Oh, why do you come and torment me in this way?"

"Perhaps because I know it does you good, Rachel. See how much better you are now than when I came in. Your eyes are sparkling with life and you've some colour in your cheeks." He drew a careless finger down my face. "You must admit that I'm right, even if you don't wish to."

"Oh, go away," I cried. "Mrs. Ramsden says I've got to rest and here you are, disturbing me and—Oh, go away, please."

Yet when he went immediately on my words, I was sorry. Because aggravating though he was, he was somebody to talk to, to fight with rather, and even that was better than being left alone.

For even though I disliked him, I told myself, with his tall well-built body and broad shoulders and that arrogant "don't care for anybody" walk of his, he made me feel safe and comfortable when he was there.

And since yesterday I, who had never consciously been afraid until I had come to Clifton Manor, had started at every shadow.

Last night Meg had stayed with me, but I knew I could not ask her to do so again, although with every bit of me I wished that I could. It was cowardly of me but I made up my mind that when Mrs. Ramsden came I would mention it to her.

Yet when she did come I could not, because the first words she said were:

"Well, you see I'm alone, Miss Rachel. Poor Meg couldn't keep her eyes open so I've sent her off to bed. Now, let me see if I can settle you comfortably for the night."

I kept her with me as long as I could, but after she had brushed and plaited my hair and made up the fire, I had to let her go.

I lay in my bed listening with concentration, but there was no sound anywhere. It was as if I was alone in a wilderness. At last I got up cautiously and went over to the door, meaning to turn the key in the lock, but it was not there. Quickly I pulled the door open, thinking it might be in the keyhole outside, but there was no sign of it.

I stood until my feet were chilled by the cold draught blowing around them, though not as chilled as my spirits were. Where could it have gone to? Surely Jason could not have taken it as he went out? Yet why should he have done that?

I frowned, trying to remember when I had last seen it but had no recollection of it after I had opened the door to let Meg in.

I looked around worriedly, knowing that unless I secured the door I would not be able to rest, then heaved a sigh of relief as my glance reached a strong-looking chair with a ladder back.

I would put the top rail of the chair-back under the door handle as I had seen Mama do once when we stayed in a strange house which she did not like. She had said then that nobody would be able to open the door without making a great noise.

I went over and picked it up, then wedged it under the handle, feeling safer and happier when I had done that. Then I climbed into bed again. I did not put out the lamp but turned the wick low so that the room was lit dimly but comfortingly.

I fell asleep almost as soon as my head touched the pillow and awoke to the sound of cocks crowing having slept undisturbed all night. I sat up gingerly and put out the lamp, then got up and padded over to the door to remove the chair, ashamed now of my fears which, in the morning light, seemed both stupid and cowardly.

For what possible harm could befall me within my grandfather's house among friends? Surely Jason must be right and my fall had really been accidental.

It was only when I got back into bed that I realized that although my shoulder was still stiff and sore, the intense pain had left it and I could move a little more freely.

I knew who I had to thank for that. Mrs. Ramsden's constant ministrations, the hot water bathings and applications of arnica had effected a swift cure. I pushed my nightgown off my shoulder. The dark, angry-looking bruise seemed to have faded a little, and I thought I would get up as soon as I could. Then, perhaps, I could go and see Philip instead of waiting for him to come to me.

When Mrs. Ramsden came in later I told her of my intention, though not the real reason for it.

She looked at me, her eyes troubled.

"I wish you wouldn't, Miss Rachel. Give yourself another day in bed, my dear. Just to please me. Meg and I are glad to take care of you and maybe by tomorrow Lizzie will have finished your new dress."

I hesitated, wanting to please her when she had been so very kind to me; then she added something which sent all my good intentions to the wind.

"Mr. Jason thinks you'd be all the better for staying in your room for another day, too."

That settled the whole matter as far as I was concerned. I had had enough of his attempts to run my life for me and this was one time when I was not going to allow it.

"No," I said firmly. "I'm well enough to go downstairs now, but I won't go outside. I promise you that, Mrs. Ramsden."

She accepted my decision after a little more argument though I could see she was not happy about it. And, to be truthful, as I went slowly down the staircase about an hour later, I was already beginning to wish I had listened to her more attentively. Because as I descended, holding tightly to the banister rail, I felt pain in muscles I never knew I had and which had been wrenched as I rolled down into the ha-ha.

Then everything became worthwhile when the front door opened and Philip came in, dressed in riding clothes, and threw his hat, gloves and crop on to the table.

There was a heavy frown between his eyes. It was the first time I had ever seen him frowning and with a shock I realized how very like his mother he was. I stopped on the stairs, looking down at him, wondering what could have disturbed him enough to make him scowl like that, and as if drawn by my intent gaze, he looked up and saw me.

Immediately the frown disappeared and

the radiant smile I was more familiar with lighted up his face.

"Rachel! Is it really you?"

He came running up the stairs and put his arm around me, hugging me to him and hurting me quite a lot. Though I would not have complained if the pain had been twenty times as bad.

"Ought you to be up? Are you well enough?"

"Yes, of course, Philip," I said, warmed by his concern. "Anyway, I was lonely upstairs by myself and—"

"You must sit down. You don't look very robust, my dear."

Gently he helped me down the remainder of the stairs and fussed over me until I was settled to his satisfaction in one of the big plush chairs.

After Jason's matter-of-fact treatment of my accident and his assumption that I was strong enough to overcome anything, it was very pleasant to be looked after as if I was a piece of Dresden china, and it made me feel precious and needed.

"Now, tell me what happened," he said, pulling up a chair and sitting beside me. "Thea told me you were confined to your

135

room and I would have liked to come and see for myself how you were, but I have been away, making arrangements to give up my legal studies, so I wasn't able to."

"Giving up your studies? But why, Philip?"

He made a comical gesture.

"What else can I do? I've no money now, Rachel, nor any prospect of having any, and legal studies are expensive."

"That isn't true! Just because I was made heir instead of you doesn't mean that you are destitute. Everything will go on as it has always done."

He pressed my hand gratefully.

"How kind of you, dear Rachel, but it is out of the question. I cannot become your pensioner, you know."

"You would not. I want to make you my co-heir." Then when he shook his head sadly, I cried, "It is my money. Surely I can dispose of it as I wish?"

"That's just what you cannot do. Didn't Mr. Lacey explain about the Trust your grandfather set up?"

"Yes, he did say something about it but I didn't really understand. What is it?"

"I only heard about it yesterday. Appar-

136

ently under the old will a Trust was set up with named Trustees. Jason's father and Lacey were appointed with the proviso that should one of them die, the other could appoint another trustee in his place. Lacey has appointed Jason as the second trustee in place of his father, so you see, Rachel—"

I stared at him, trying to understand the import of what he had said, but without success.

"No, I don't, Philip. What difference does it make?"

"All the difference in the world. Under the Trust you will only receive the income for life. You can't touch the capital, therefore you can't share your inheritance with me, and—as I said—I will not become your pensioner."

"But if I tell them that is what I want them to do," I said eagerly.

He shook his head.

"Do you think Jason would agree? He has no love for either me or Thea, make no mistake about that."

"I can't believe that, Philip."

He laughed then, some of the strain leaving his face.

"Thank you, dear Rachel, for saying that. Nevertheless it's true. Jason and I have never hit it off together, I'm afraid. I expect it's my fault, though I have tried—"

He stopped and shrugged helplessly and I put out my hand to him impulsively.

"I am sure you have, Philip. How could you do otherwise? Is there no way round?"

"Only one. When you marry the Trust will be broken for then your property passes to your husband. If only—"

I felt my pulses begin to beat unevenly and willed him to go on, to say the words I wanted to hear. When he did not I asked breathlessly:

"If only what?"

He got up and moved away from me.

"Nothing, Rachel. It's too soon. Perhaps one day—I must go, little cousin. Thea will be watching for me this hour, to know how I managed." He came back and took my hand in his, pressing it gently. "Thank you for what you have said. It's a great comfort to me to know that you are my friend."

He left me on those words, running up the staircase two at a time, leaving me confused but filled with an irrational happiness.

I tried to tell myself I was foolish, was reading into his broken sentences more than he intended, but it was to no avail. His words had given me hope that one day my dreams of love and ecstasy with the husband of my choice would come true, and I gazed into the heart of the fire, dreaming of a wonderful future with Philip.

It was Meg who roused me from my happy state, running into the hall from the kitchen premises saying:

"Miss Rachel, the gypsy's here. Will you see her?"

"Yes, of course, Meg," I said eagerly. "What is she selling?"

"She's only got pegs and firewood this time, so we weren't going to bother you. Only she asked to see you."

"Asked to see me?"

"Yes. It's right queer, Miss. She told my fortune and Mrs. Ramsden's, then says she, 'Isn't there another young lady here? A stranger? Bring her to me.' So I came to see, Miss."

I got up.

"I'll come through to the kitchen, Meg. How strange she should know I'm here. Though maybe she's heard from one of the other houses—"

When I went in to the kitchen a tall woman, with black hair hanging straight down around her shoulders got up from a wooden chair beside the table. She was dressed in tawdry but colourful and vaguely outlandish clothes. Her skin was swarthy and she had magnificent brilliant eyes which seemed to bore right into me as she turned to face me.

"This is her, Miss Rachel," Meg said unnecessarily.

I smiled and greeted the woman calmly enough, even though that steady gaze was making me feel strangely fearful.

She did not reply to my greeting but stood there, looking at me out of those brilliant eyes for quite a long time. Then she said at last in a deep, harsh voice:

"Sit down, Miss, and I'll set out the cards."

I did as she said and watched as her brown hands moved the cards about on the table as if I was mesmerized.

"What do you see?" I asked at last.

"There can be great happiness for you in this place, Miss, but the cards are dark. Take heed for there is danger all around you."

"Danger? What danger?"

"I cannot tell, but beware the white horseman, the deep dark water. Beware the smiling face that hides your bitter enemy."

"I don't understand. What water? Who is my enemy?"

"The cards do not tell me that. They only show the smiling face which hides a black heart. Beware!" she said again. "Or death will find and smite you."

She swept the cards together with those words and without warning strode to the door and pulled it open, closing it behind her before any of us could move. Then we ran to the window and watched her walk through the yard and begin to climb the hill at the back of the house with a free and swinging stride which carried her along at a great rate, until she disappeared into a wood which hid the top of the hill from the house.

I returned to the table and sank into a chair, feeling weak and full of trouble.

"What did she mean?" I said, looking from Mrs. Ramsden to Meg and back again.

"Oh, Miss, it must be like the white lady that haunts the old mine up yonder," Meg said, almost babbling with fear. "That's why my Eddie always comes to meet me on my Sunday off, in case—"

"Nonsense," Mrs. Ramsden contradicted bracingly. "That's an old wives' tale. Take no notice of her, Miss Rachel, and as for that gypsy, well they love to foretell trouble and danger. I'd pay no attention to her."

"But it's true! Eddie's missus says people have seen the white lady before today and she's always brought them death and disaster. Eh, I'm affeared for Miss Rachel."

"Meg, I won't tell you again," the housekeeper snapped.

I pulled myself together with an effort, knowing I must throw off the effects of the gypsy's melodramatic predictions and at the same time reassure both Meg and myself.

"Don't fret, Meg," I said as cheerfully as I could. "Mrs. Ramsden is right. These people try to gain ascendancy over us by frightening us. She's probably heard the legend of the white lady and has tried to improve on it. You must forget about it, as I mean to."

"Quite right, too," Mrs. Ramsden agreed. "Now, Meg, you've plenty to do before supper. Away with you or you'll never be finished." She waited until Meg had left the kitchen, then went on anxiously, "Are you sure you're all right, Miss Rachel? If I'd known that gypsy would say such things I'd never have let her see you."

"Yes, don't worry, Mrs. Ramsden." I got up and moved towards the door. "I'll go back into the hall and leave you to get on with your work. I've already forgotten all the silly superstitious nonsense she told me."

But I had not. In spite of my brave words I did not find it so easy to shake off the foreboding which the gypsy had aroused in me, nor the effect of that burning gaze and the flash of the heavy ring she wore on her forefinger as she lifted her hand in warning.

Beware the deep dark water, she had

said. Beware the white horseman and the enemy with the smiling face. Surely it was only the usual claptrap that kind of person talked to gain effect?

Yet there had already been an attack on me although Jason had tried to tell me I was mistaken. Jason who, as Thea had said, had found me so opportunely in the ha-ha. Though nobody could accuse him of having a smiling face for me. On the contrary!

Then I remembered his smile, which though infrequent lighted his face, making him seem a different person altogether, and I was afraid.

8

I HAD not sat alone for long, brooding and hoping Philip would soon return, beside the fire in the great hall, when Jason came in through the side door and checked at the sight of me.

"Rachel! Surely you shouldn't be downstairs already?"

I roused myself to answer him normally.

"Yes. I feel very much better today and thought I ought to make the effort."

He stood beside me, frowning down at me.

"You look very pale and tired. Mrs. Ramsden should have forbidden you—"

"She had no choice," I interrupted. "I wanted to come downstairs. Though I don't intend to stay up for very much longer," I added honestly, because the session with the gypsy woman had made me feel excessively weary.

"I'm sure you're wise." He picked up a box which he had placed on the floor beside him and put it on my knee. "I saw this today and thought you might like it. I hope you will."

"What is it?" I asked, looking down with pleasure at the box tied with pretty ribbons.

"Open it and see."

I did as he suggested, carefully untying the ribbon, then lifting the lid and turning back the paper which covered the contents. I lifted them out, hardly able to believe my eyes. He had brought me a necklet and huge muff in white fur, decorated with little black tails.

"Jason, how lovely! It's just like the one I saw that day. Oh, I can't believe it's true!"

I lifted the muff to my face, holding it against me, feeling so pleased and excited that I could not say any more. Then, abruptly, commonsense returned and I put the muff down slowly.

"But I can't have it," I said hopelessly. "It's far too expensive. There won't be any of my fifty pounds left if I buy these as well."

He smiled, his face lighting up as it always did.

"Certainly there will be, Rachel. That

isn't an expensive fur, you know. You'll still have plenty of pin money left if you decide to keep your muff. I thought you'd be pleased to have it."

"I am," I said quickly, feeling my face reddening at the reproach in his voice. "I shall hate to part with it."

"Then why do so when there's no need? Please keep it, Rachel. I'd like you to have it."

"As long as you're sure it doesn't leave me in debt. Mama always had a horror of owing money, and I suppose I've inherited it."

"That's not a bad thing to inherit, but I do assure you that this purchase hasn't bankrupted you."

"Then I'll certainly keep it." I cuddled the soft fur against my face again. "Thank you for getting them for me."

"You've nothing to thank me for," he said with all his old abruptness. Then added persuasively, "Don't you think you should go to your room now, Rachel? I feel sure you've been up long enough for one day."

"Yes, perhaps you're right." I got up, still clutching my necklet and muff, and

Jason put his hand under my arm and helped me up the staircase.

"I'll send Mrs. Ramsden to you," he said when we reached my room. "I'm glad to see you up and about again, Rachel. Take care of yourself, my dear."

"I will, and thank you for your kindness," I said shyly and went into my room.

When Mrs. Ramsden came I was standing in front of the mirror, the fur necklet in place and my hands tucked inside the huge white muff.

"Why, Miss Rachel," she said, "where did you get them from?"

"Mr. Jason brought them for me. It isn't an expensive set, Mrs. Ramsden, but I like it all the more for that. I've always wanted one and now I can hardly believe it's true."

"Did Mr. Jason say it wasn't expensive?" she asked, in rather a strange voice.

"Yes." I looked at her in surprise. "Why?"

"Well, if he said it, then it must be so," she said. "Now, Miss Rachel, come and I'll help you to undress."

I put my muff down on the dressing-table with reluctance, even though I knew I would be glad to lie down on my bed, because I felt exhausted by the events of that day, only half listening as the housekeeper chatted while she ministered to me.

"I did tell Mrs. Morley I'd be moving you into the Master's room today," she said as she pulled my nightgown over my head, "but I think you'll be as well in here till you've got over your fall."

"Oh, yes," I answered fervently. "I love this room, Mrs. Ramsden. I'd as soon stay here for ever if I could."

"Mrs. Morley thinks you should have the best bedroom and so does Mr. Philip, but it can wait a few days. Here comes Meg with the hot water. Now I'll bathe your bruises, my dear, and put some more arnica on them. They're coming along nicely, I'm pleased to say."

When I was tucked in bed and she was about to leave me to see to the evening meal, I remembered the strange disappearance of the door key.

"Mrs. Ramsden," I said quickly. "I thought there was a key to this room but when I looked for it last night it wasn't there. Have you seen it?"

"No, my dear. It ought to be there. Now where—" She opened the door and looked outside. "Why, here it is! All safe and sound. Somebody's left it on the outside, that's all." She fitted it into the keyhole on the room side and smiled across at me. "I must get on, Miss Rachel. Meg'll bring you something to eat just as soon as she can."

"Thank you," I said mechanically, and as soon as she had gone, got out of bed and hurried over to the door. I took the key out of the keyhole and carried it back to the bed, hiding it carefully under the pillow, ready to use later on.

For I knew very well it had not been there last night. Somebody had replaced it since then, but who? And why had it been taken in the first place?

I did not know the answers to those questions, but its strange reappearance brought back my fears with increased violence and I wished passionately that there was somebody at Clifton Manor to whom I could impart them and who would not laugh me to scorn.

But there was nobody. Philip, I knew, would listen to me sympathetically but I did not want to add to his burdens. He had worries enough of his own connected with his future. And Jason—

A picture of his strong, dark face rose in my mind. There was no doubt that he would be able to give me the reassurance I needed so badly, yet I could not seek his help.

Because although to Meg I had made little of the gypsy's prophecy, to myself I had to admit that her words had impressed themselves on me with frightening impact.

So that while I acknowledged that Jason was a man who was probably afraid of nothing in the world, yet I could not turn to him. In case I was asking for aid from the very person who was trying to encompass my ruin.

The thought was out now and I did not flinch from it any longer, remembering what both Philip and his mother had hinted to me. And I knew myself, had known from the very first moment I had seen him, that in spite of his kindly impulses, he was a man of implacable resolve who would not lightly turn away from anything he had determined should be done.

By the time Meg brought me my evening meal, my mind was made up. Somehow I had to find the gypsy woman and force her to tell me what she had meant, who was the person I had to fear, what the danger was that threatened me.

Then if she refused, I would know that it was only a tale to frighten the credulous and I would reject it.

I had half hoped that Philip might have come to see me now that he knew I was not ill, but the evening dragged away until Meg came to pick up my tray and to make up the fire for the night.

I would have liked to have kept her with me but I knew I could not. She had other duties to perform and would have little enough time to call her own before going up to her little attic bedroom. And although the room was bright with the lamplight, it seemed to become darker when she had gone.

I got up almost at once and locked the door, taking the key back to bed with me and hiding it again under my pillow. Then I turned down the lamp carefully so that there was still a tiny glow of light and got back into bed, hoping that the events of the day and the prophecies of the gypsy woman would not result in either sleeplessness or nightmares.

But I need not have worried. My last conscious thought was of Jason's kindness in bringing me my lovely muff, and I knew no more until I woke to find it full daylight once again. I had slept quietly and dreamlessly, disturbed neither by nocturnal visitors nor by horrifying fantasies.

I had risen and unlocked the door before Meg brought me my breakfast and had been pleased to find that I could move more freely, almost without pain.

"How are you feeling this morning, Miss Rachel?" she asked, pulling back the curtains with a rattle.

"Very much better, thank you. I think I'll get up as soon as I've eaten."

"You'd better wait till Mrs. Ramsden sees you, Miss. She'll want to make sure you're really well enough."

"All right," I said, though I had no intention of letting either the housekeeper or anybody else keep me from following the resolution I had made last night. Though I did not set out as early as I had hoped.

Because after Mrs. Ramsden had left me after helping me to dress, Lizzie came in with my new dress and mantle and I had to try them on. First the black dress with its fitted bodice fastened by tiny velvet buttons, and finished with a white lace frill at neck and sleeve ends and bands of velvet around the full, sweeping skirt. Then the hip-length mantle to match.

Lizzie was quite right. Black threw into relief my red hair and made my skin look whiter than ever, and I postured in front of the mirror admiring myself, until I remembered why I was wearing that colour.

Then I came to my senses and was ashamed because I had forgotten Mama so easily, even though I knew she would have been glad that I was enjoying my new clothes.

I showed Lizzie my new muff and necklet and she agreed that they looked magnificent with my new clothes. When I told her who had chosen them and how cheaply he had bought them, she only said, with a shake of her head:

"Aye, that's like Mr. Jason. He's the kindest and most thoughtful man you'd meet in a day's march, so he is," and I smiled to myself at her staunch support of the man she had known from his infancy, and could sympathize with her even while I did not agree.

Then Lizzie carefully placed the pretty little hat she had made for me on the plaits which Mrs. Ramsden had wound around my head and I whispered to myself, "Don't I look nice, Mama?" and somehow felt sure that she was happy for me.

It was not until I had eaten the light luncheon which Meg brought to my room, saying that nobody else was in, that I at last went downstairs, dressed in my new finery and carrying my muff.

As I went down the staircase and across the hall, the Manor seemed to be deserted and as silent as the grave. I shivered slightly as I opened the side door and stepped out on to the path, leaving the house and walking across the rose garden to find the way which would lead to the trees above the Manor into which the gypsy had disappeared.

It was quite a stiff climb and took me longer than I had expected. Certainly a good deal longer than it had taken the gypsy with her long, swinging stride.

When I at last reached the wood I leaned for a while against a tree until my heart and lungs were functioning normally again. I could hear the birds twittering and the soft rustles as small animals went about their business, but no sound which might indicate the presence of a gypsy camp. Not the stamp or whinny of a horse, nor the bark of a dog.

After I had rested I set out along a path which was clearly defined and quite dry because the weather had been fine though dull since I had come to Clifton Manor. Every few yards I stopped to listen, but could not hear the sounds I hoped for.

I must have covered quite a lot of ground as I rambled up and down paths, meeting nobody, seeing and hearing no other human being.

At last I came to a small clearing and examined it carefully, looking for the traces gypsies always left behind them when they encamped anywhere, but without success. Then I became aware of the sound of running water and went towards it eagerly, because surely if there was a camp anywhere, it would be near to a stream, but again there were no signs of it.

I walked beside it for as long as I could, holding up my skirt to keep it from the leaves which lay thickly on the banks. Then when the bushes encroached very close to the water, I had to strike up among the trees again.

Eventually I came to a narrow ride and was glad to find a fallen tree on which I could rest. I spread my handkerchief over it and sat down, beginning to feel weary and despondent and to suspect I had come on a fruitless journey.

I looked around me, wondering if it was worthwhile going on, afraid that once I was out of hearing of the murmur of the running water I might not easily find my way back. Then I saw that straight in front of me the trees thinned and there seemed to be a patch of open land.

I would just go as far as that, I told myself, and make sure the camp was not there, then I would follow the stream back to where I had left the first path.

I got up and went quickly to the edge of the trees, then stopped in surprise. In front of me, stretching across the clearing as if a giant axe had made a long cleft in the ground, was a huge crevice.

I walked towards it cautiously, holding on to a broken tree stump as I neared the edge, looking down with a shudder. For the cleft was very deep, with almost perpendicular sides. And at the bottom, glistening evilly, was a mere, still and dark, without a ripple to break its surface.

The whole place seemed silent, a menacing silence which made me catch my breath, filling me with a stabbing fear. There was no sound to be heard. No rustle of trees or bushes, no bird noises. It was as if every living thing had deserted this place, had fled from it because of the frightening emanations which made my limbs tremble and my fingers cling ever more tightly to the tree stump in case I went hurtling down into those dark depths.

It was then, at the lowest ebb of my courage, that I heard the hoofbeats coming towards me through trees which looked quite impenetrable. I straightened up, still clinging to the tree, peering through the gathering gloom, and the fear I had known was as nothing to that which seized me now.

Beware the white horseman, the gypsy had said, fixing me with her burning eye. Beware the dark water.

I could not move a limb even though my brain shrieked for me to get away, to run back into the wood and hide, as the inexorable hoofbeats came nearer and nearer.

Then as a horse came bursting out of the dark trees at the other end of the pit my legs at last obeyed the dictates of my brain and I pulled myself back from the deadly brink and stumbled towards the path.

There was a shout and I had a vision of flashing hooves over my head before I fell to the ground, hearing the trampling of the horse about me, able to do nothing but wait for what must be the inevitable end.

Then I was roughly pulled to my feet and shaken hard, while Jason's angry voice sounded in my ears.

"What the devil do you think you're doing, terrifying my horse like that! Don't you know better than to appear suddenly out of nowhere? We might have all gone over the side."

He shook me again but I was beyond caring what he did. I could only cling to him in weak relief because I had been rescued from that terrible fear which had paralysed me.

"Jason! I'm so glad it's only you. I thought it was the white horseman come for me!"

He shook me again, though more gently this time.

"Pull yourself together, Rachel. What are you talking about? And what are you doing up here at this time of day?"

I stood up straight, still feeling weak and faint but responding to the commanding note in his voice.

"I came to find the gypsy."

He frowned.

"What gypsy?"

"The one who came yesterday and told my fortune. She said to beware of the white horseman and the dark water. This place—it terrifed me, Jason. Then I heard your horse and I thought—"

"Do I look like a white horseman?" he said in his usual blighting way.

And when I looked into his dark face with the black crisp hair curling round it, I had to admit how foolish I had been.

"But it is a dreadful place," I insisted, shuddering again although I was no longer alone. "There's something menacing about it, as if some terrible thing has happened here."

"You're too imaginative, Rachel. Come. I'll take you home."

He picked up my muff which I had dropped in my fear, and brushed the skirt of my dress with his hand. Then he mounted his horse which had been quietly cropping the grass and swung me up in front of him as if I had been a feather weight, holding me close against him as the horse began to canter along the ride.

I leaned back, feeling his arm strong and heavy about me and, strangely enough, gaining comfort from it and a diminution of the horror that had gripped me so short a while ago.

He said nothing until we arrived in the stable yard. Then he dismounted and lifted me down from the horse.

"Go in by the side door," he said curtly. "Go straight to your room. I'll come as soon as I've seen Star bestowed. Tell nobody about this."

I meekly did as he ordered because there was nothing I wanted more than the quiet and seclusion of my own room. Nor could I then have talked to anybody about that terrifying period while those steady, seemingly menacing hoofbeats had come irrevocably closer to me.

I was shivering when I reached my room and went to stand in front of the fire, holding out my hands to its warmth. I was still in the same place when Jason came in, his face stern and bleak.

"Will you never learn sense, Rachel?" he said harshly, as he closed the door. Then as he saw me properly his expression softened.

"My poor child." He came closer to me, taking my hands in his and chafing them comfortingly. "I didn't realize. What frightened you so much?"

"I don't know. I thought—" My fingers clung tightly to his. "It was that place. As if somebody had been murdered there."

"Perhaps he had," he murmured, so quietly that I barely caught the words.

"What do you mean?"

"That was the place where your Grandfather was found."

I stared at him, shocked by his words, and saw a bleak spasm of pain twist his mouth.

"Grandfather?" I repeated.

He nodded, his hands, warming and strong, tightening on mine.

"He and his horse were found at the bottom of that pit. Both dead," he said sombrely.

I was silent, trying to adjust to this unexpected answer, realizing now that I had half-known about this tragedy.

"But surely it was an accident? Not—not murder!"

He stared at me broodingly.

"Perhaps. Who knows? I thought it was going to be repeated when you suddenly materialized in front of us and Star reared. You do realize that we might both have gone crashing over the edge?"

"I do now. I didn't think, Jason. I only wanted to get away—"

He put his hand on my head and stroked my hair gently.

"It's all right, Rachel. There was no

harm done, as it happens. Only promise me one thing, will you?"

I looked at him, my cheeks wet with tears I made no attempt to stem.

"You know I will."

He smiled.

"How docile that sounds. Not a bit in keeping with this lovely hair. Promise me you won't go wandering off by yourself any more. If you must go out walking, take Meg with you."

"But she has her work to do."

"I'll see Mrs. Ramsden and arrange for her to be released to accompany you. She can easily hire another girl to help her. Will you do that?"

"Yes, I will. I promise. Thank you, Jason."

"Thank *you*," he said gravely. "Now, tidy yourself up and come down to supper, Rachel. You and I may both be excused from changing our dress tonight, I think. Anyway, your new gown is very becoming to you. Au revoir, my dear."

When he had gone I sat down beside the fire, looking back over what had happened, wishing I could stay quietly in my room for the rest of the evening. But I knew I must not.

Jason had commanded that I should go down and I must do so, if only to show him how grateful I was for his help and kindness, to demonstrate my regret because I had so nearly caused a tragedy. But only the thought of seeing Philip again made the coming hours seem bearable to me.

9

EVEN though I wanted so much to see Philip, it was still an effort to leave my bedroom and go downstairs to join the others, and it was with a deep sense of disappointment that I found only Thea and Jason in the great hall. Perhaps he would come soon, I told myself hopefully, but my hopes were very soon dashed.

"So you're better, Rachel," Thea said languidly from the sofa. "I told Philip he need not worry about you, and see how right I was."

"Where is he?" Jason asked, putting into words the question I wanted to know the answer to so badly.

"Poor boy. He's gone to try and fnd some way of earning a living. This stupid will—"

"But he knows there's no need for that," I cried. "I've already told him I'll continue the allowances Grandfather made to you both. And when I can,

I mean to settle part of the estate on him."

"You'll do nothing of the kind," Jason cut in firmly.

I whirled to face him.

"Why not? Surely I can do what I like with my own, once everything is properly settled."

"You can't. Eventually you will receive an income from the estate. Naturally nobody can stop you doing anything you desire with that money, but you can't divide the property."

"You mean you won't allow me to," I said resentfully.

"Mr. Lacey and I hold the estate in trust, Rachel. We have no authority to carve it up, even if we wished to."

"But if Rachel should marry?" Thea's softly voiced question brought our eyes round to her. "Wouldn't her husband then be able to break the Trust?"

"He might," Jason answered, "but such an application would only be considered if you married with your Trustees' consent, Rachel. Naturally it would not be un-reasonably withheld but we would have to be very sure you were not intending to marry an adventurer—a fortune hunter."

I thought of the man I wanted to marry —Philip, my Apollo, with the fair and open countenance. Nobody could accuse him of being a fortune hunter, that was certain. If only my dream could come true, then all his problems would be solved.

Then I remembered Miss Ainsworth and knew that there was no hope for me. For why should he ever think of me when he could marry her, beautiful and rich as she was?

"Such a disgraceful state of affairs." Thea's complaining voice disturbed my thoughts and brought me back from my dreams. "I do think Tobias might have made a proper will before he died."

"Perhaps he didn't expect to die just at that time," Jason said curtly.

She shrugged.

"At his age he should have been prepared. He always said Philip would be his heir, but instead he made a pauper of my poor boy and ruined all his prospects."

Jason's lips tightened but before he could reply Mrs. Ramsden came to tell us supper was ready. He bent and picked up

"She certainly is. Where are you going?"

"We are taking Lizzie to meet her son and intend to enjoy the air at the same time."

"May I accompany you?"

"Oh, I'm not sure. Lizzie—" I stammered, the prospect of being with him delighting me, even while I did not want to offend Lizzie by not going with her as I had promised. But she soon reassured me.

"There's no need for you to come, Miss Rachel," she said. "Meg will go with me, won't you, girl?"

"Yes, and you'll be all right with Mr. Philip, that I'm sure of."

"Then that's settled." Philip took my hand in his and tucked it under his arm. "Come and tell me everything that's happened since I left the Manor yesterday morning."

I picked up my skirt in my free hand, glad that I had left on the modish black skirt lavishly trimmed with braid, and the lace-trimmed white blouse and fitted jacket which Lizzie had brought with her and finished during the morning.

172

Thea, carrying her into the dining-room and putting her into the chair she usually occupied.

Nothing more was said about Grandfather or about my inheritance while Mrs. Ramsden was with us, and what conversation there was seemed dull and spasmodic. We needed Philip to liven us up with his gaiety, but he had still not returned when we went back into the hall after our meal.

Jason left us as soon as he had put Thea on to the sofa and I soon followed him, making my excuses to Thea. I was feeling now the reaction from my fruitless quest for the gypsy and from the very real fears which had consumed me.

My bedroom, with its blazing fire and candle and lamp light looked very welcoming and homely when I went in, and I was glad Mrs. Ramsden had still not moved me into Grandfather's old room which would be, I was sure, too big and grand for me.

I sat for a while by the fire, luxuriating in its warmth and in a manner of life which was very new to me, before undressing. When I was ready for bed I

169

took the key from its hiding place under my pillow and was about to lock the door when Mrs. Ramsden opened it.

"Why, Miss Rachel, I came to help you but I see I'm not needed," she exclaimed.

"I'm so much better, thanks to you, that I was able to manage by myself."

"That's good news. You're sure you've everything you want?"

"Yes, thank you."

"Then I'll say goodnight, Miss Rachel. God bless you. Sleep well," she said and left me comforted by her words.

I locked the door securely behind her, then snuffed the candles and turned down the lamp before climbing into bed and falling at once into a deep and dreamless sleep, my last conscious thought being of Philip and how much I looked forward to seeing him tomorrow.

Though it was quite late in the afternoon before I did so. All the morning Lizzie had been with me and between us, with some help from Meg, we had finished the filmy gown which I hoped to wear for the first time that evening. There was also a white lace shawl to put round my shoulders if I felt cold and an ornament to

match to wear in my hair, both of wh[ich] Lizzie had made out of some of [the] material Jason had brought.

Jason must have seen Mrs. Rams[den] about releasing Meg to be with me beca[use] Lizzie said she had brought her daught[er,] youngest girl to help and nobody c[ame] looking for Meg, as they would have d[one] usually.

When Lizzie was ready to go ho[me] Meg and I decided to take her as fa[r as] the farm gate where her son would m[eet] her with the cart. As we came out of [the] bedroom we saw Philip standing at the [foot] of the stairs. He had his back to us [and] when I called to him he turned round [and] came to us.

"You're back at last," I said happil[y.]

"I've just arrived. I went to see [Tabby] but she was resting and her dragon [of a] maid wouldn't let me in. I was wonde[ring] if I might find you, Rachel. You're loo[king] very lovely."

I blushed at the unmistakable ad[mir]ation in his eyes.

"Lizzie's been making me some [new] clothes, as you can see. She's very clev[er."]

Because no matter what one's troubles might be, one could not help feeling pleased that one looked one's very best when going for a stroll with a man like Philip.

By the time we reached the side door and went out into the garden, I had completely forgotten Meg and Lizzie and was only aware of the man beside me.

"Philip," I said as we strolled along, "your mother said last night that you'd gone away to find yourself paid employment. Why did you do that after what I said to you?"

His fingers tightened on mine.

"It was because of that, Rachel. Ah, if only you could understand—"

"I would like to, Philip. Won't you explain?"

"How can I? It is too soon. You would hardly believe me—"

"Not believe you!" I laughed at the idea. "I can't imagine that happening."

He stopped and turned to face me, taking my hands in his.

"Don't you know what I'm trying to say? Haven't you seen? Rachel, don't you understand what I'm telling you?"

I shook my head dumbly even while a sharp stab of rapture ripped through me. Yet surely I must have misunderstood? Philip could not possibly mean what I thought, what I hoped with all my heart was the truth.

His hands slid up my arms and he pulled me closer to him.

"Rachel, I think it happened the very first moment I saw you. I stood on the stairs, looking down at you. Then you turned and smiled at me and I knew at once."

"What did you know?" I asked breathlessly, feeling a pulse begin to hammer in my throat.

"I knew I loved you. Without hearing you speak, without knowing a thing about you, I knew you were my girl. But I ought not to have spoken to you yet. I will frighten you away, my timid little bird."

I was aware of his strong fingers biting into my arms yet I felt no pain. I could only look at him, into his pleading blue eyes, and try to believe that what I had heard him say was not a dream, as surely it must be.

"Philip," I said and swayed towards him.

I felt his arms go round me, then I was crushed against him and he was kissing me. And instead of pushing him away as I should have done, I was kissing him back as if I had waited all my life for that moment. As indeed I had.

Then as suddenly as he had caught me to him, he thrust me away and covered his eyes with his hands.

"Philip! What is it? What's wrong?"

He groaned.

"Can you ever forgive me, Rachel? I meant to be strong, to love you in secret, never to let you know. For what have I to offer you? Nothing. A man without prospects, without money, and you an heiress. What must you be thinking of me?"

I sighed with relief, now that I knew what was worrying him and how easily I might reassure him.

"As though that mattered, Philip. Whatever I have is all yours. I want to share it with you, you know that. Oh, I realize that while we're both in mourning nothing can be said, but it's wonderful to know you love me, as I love you."

The last words I spoke so quietly that I thought—perhaps hoped—he would not hear them, but he did and his face lit up with happiness. But this time he did not touch me.

"Rachel, that's the most miraculous thing that's ever happened to me, to know you love me. But you are right. However I may hate it, this must be our secret until the time is ripe to let everyone know. Even Thea."

"But she's your mother. Surely you should tell her?"

He shook his head, his eyes bright with happiness.

"Not yet. One day, perhaps, when I've got used to the wonder of knowing you love me, I'll tell her. But for now I want it to be our special secret. Yours and mine. Something that will bind us together with silken strands."

"All right, Philip. It shall be just as you wish."

"Give me one last kiss, Rachel, then I must go and see if Thea is awake. Till later, my dearest love."

His lips brushed mine and then he was gone, leaving me standing in a golden dream, going over and over the events of the past minutes.

It did not seem possible that Philip should love me. That through pain and loss I should have at last found the man I had dreamed of ever since I was old enough to have such dreams. And I had foolishly thought he loved Elaine. How stupid I had been.

I was so lost in my plans for our future that Meg was upon me before I even heard her coming.

"Where's Mr. Philip?" she demanded. "He said he was taking you for a walk."

"He had to go back into the house, Meg."

"Lucky for me Mr. Jason didn't come home and find you all by yourself then," she scolded. "I'd have been in real trouble, so I would, for neglecting my orders."

"But he didn't come, so everything's all right," I said gaily, trying to coax her out of her ill-humour. "Let us take a little stroll about the garden before we go in. Was Lizzie's son waiting for her?"

"Yes he was, so I was able to come back to you. And a good thing, too, finding you by yourself like this."

I could see that she was still seriously put about so I forbore to tease her any further. Instead I said reasonably:

"You can't be with me all the time, Meg. Sometimes you'll have your day off."

She nodded seriously.

"I know, and it's on Sunday. I wondered if I didn't ought to let it go this time, but Mr. Jason said no, because it only comes once a month."

"I should think not indeed. I'll have you remember I'm not a baby, Meg."

"I know that, Miss Rachel, but there's nothing to worry about. Mr. Jason says he'll take care of you when I'm not there."

I pulled a face.

"Very kind of him, I'm sure."

She looked at me sharply.

"Now don't you go getting in a pet at Mr. Jason. He doesn't want to find you out of your senses at the bottom of the ha-ha again and no more do I. He's only thinking of your good, Miss Rachel."

"I suppose so. Where are you going on Sunday?"

"To the farm where Eddie works. He's my friend. He's going to meet me by the old mine, up yonder. I said I'd be there by four o'clock. I hope I won't have to keep him waiting."

"Four o'clock? But you said it was your day off."

"So it is. I can go as soon as I've finished my work, as long as I'm back by nine to do the bedroom fires and the hot water. Though Mrs. Ramsden's very good. She never minds if I'm a bit late."

I was appalled, not only because poor Meg had so short a time for her "day" off but because she accepted it so uncomplainingly. One day, I told myself earnestly, when I was really in charge of Clifton Manor, I would change all that and make sure my servants were allowed better conditions and more freedom.

"Does Eddie always come to meet you?"

"Yes, when it gets dark early. Not that I'm really afraid, Miss Rachel, don't think that. It's just that it's creepy walking past that old mine. Suppose I saw the white lady, walking about and wringing her hands."

"But surely you don't really believe in that, Meg?"

"Well, it's like this, I do and I don't. Down here in the daylight, I don't, but when it's getting dark and I'm near that old mine, well I remember all the tales Eddie's mistress tells and I'm not so sure."

"Then I'm glad he meets you. Does he bring you back?"

"Just to the edge of the path, Miss Rachel. I don't mind after that."

"I see," I said slowly, and formed a resolve to tell Mrs. Ramsden that Eddie was to be allowed to bring Meg all the way home, once my inheritance was settled.

"You won't go off by yourself again, Miss Rachel?"

"No, I won't go anywhere without you or Mr. Jason."

But I didn't tell her the real reason why in future I would want her with me even when I was accompanied by Philip. Because only in that way would we be able to safeguard our secret from everybody.

The secret which filled me with so much joy and which would, in time, solve the problem of how I was going to ensure that Philip and his mother did not suffer because of my good luck.

When we went back into the house I went upstairs to my bedroom and began a leisurely toilet, putting on the new gown which Lizzie had made for me, delighting in its elegance. Yet when I was ready to go down I was suddenly afraid. How was I going to meet Philip without giving myself away? Without betraying our love which was so new and so deep. And I had to force myself to go out of the bedroom to join the others.

They were all in the hall, waiting for me. Philip had his back to me. He was sitting on the edge of the sofa talking to Thea and did not turn round. I perfectly understood his reason but could only feel sorry that nobody except Jason saw me sweep down the staircase in all my finery, with my hair in a coronet on top of my head, crowned by the ornament Lizzie had made for me, and with curly tendrils hanging down around my face.

He came to meet me, raising my gloved hand to his lips in a very gallant way.

"You look very lovely, Rachel," he said. "Lizzie has really surpassed herself this time."

Out of the corner of my eye I saw Philip give one swift secret glance at me and felt rewarded for the time and trouble I had taken over my toilet.

Thea also looked up and her eyes narrowed.

"Come over here and let me look at you," she said in her usual languid way. "Yes, very nice. Very *comme-il-faut*," and I thanked her even though I was not sure what she meant or whether she had paid me a compliment or not.

"Who made your gown, Rachel?"

"Lizzie," I said eagerly. "Jason found her for me and he bought some material out of the money Mr. Lacey gave me, and a beautiful white fur muff and necklet, too. With little black tails for ornament."

"How much did Lacey give you?"

"Fifty pounds."

"And you got all that, with an ermine—"

"White fur, Thea," Jason interrupted, his brows frowning. "A very cheap white fur."

Her lips curled and she shrugged her shoulders lightly.

"Just as you say, Jason."

I looked from one to the other, completely mystified by what was passing between them. Then I forgot about it as Thea said:

"Mrs. Ramsden tells me you haven't yet moved into your own room. Why not?"

I was taken aback at this sudden attack and said in confusion:

"I like my present room. It's very comfortable. I—"

"Perhaps so, my dear, but you mustn't be selfish, you know. You ought to consider the servants. Mrs. Ramsden and Meg have worked hard to get the other room ready for you. It's unkind of you not to change over to it now it is ready."

"I'm sorry," I stammered. "I didn't know—I'll change over tomorrow."

"Nonsense, Thea," Jason cut in. "Rachel can stay where she is. Mrs. Ramsden won't mind at all if she does."

"You're so thoughtless, Jason," Thea chided. "I'm sure Rachel knows better than to take any notice of you."

"So am I sure she does," Philip said, and smiled directly at me for the first time since I had come downstairs.

"Of course I do," I said, feeling warmed and comforted by his smile, so that for the rest of the evening I was able to enjoy being in his company, sharing our secret, feeling his love reaching out to me as if it was a tangible thing.

That night when Mrs. Ramsden came to see if I needed anything before she went to her bed, I told her I was ready to move to Grandfather's old room tomorrow, and apologized for not doing so before.

"Eh, no need to worry about that, Miss Rachel. You can sleep where you please. It's your own place, after all. Only I do think that as the mistress you ought to have old master's room."

"And so I shall, Mrs. Ramsden. Thank you for all you've done for me. I do appreciate it."

"There, my dear, it's easy enough to do things for you. You're a fine wee lassie and I'm right fond of you already."

When she had gone I sat by my fire for a while, thinking how lucky I was. I had lost Mama, that was true, and it was something I would not find easy to forget, but my lot had fallen in very pleasant places, among so many kind friends. And Mama had brought it about for me.

It was she who had written to the lawyer, who had told me what to do, who had made sure I would not be alone in the world after she had left me. And it was Mama who had found my own dear Philip for me.

I sat on, dreaming happy dreams of a future when Philip and I would be here together, with our children. I, an only child, had always insisted I would have at least six children, three boys and three girls when I married. Mama had laughed at me and said, "Wait until you see who you marry, my girl. You can't order them, you know, and they cost money to keep."

Well, I knew now who I was to marry, and would be able to afford my six children, if God granted them to us.

"Mama," I whispered, "I'm so happy. Thank you, and God bless you, my own dearest."

It was not until I had turned down the lamp and was settling down to sleep that I remembered. Here in Clifton Manor an enemy lurked, an enemy whom I had not seen but whose deadly hand I had felt.

And all the happiness and pleasure disappeared, leaving me a prey to fears for the future which were once again very real to me.

10

MRS. RAMSDEN and Meg moved my belongings into Grandfather's room the next day and when I joined them there I had to admit that it was a change for the better. Because it was a beautiful room.

Square and perfectly proportioned, with what the housekeeper said was linenfold panelling in a light kind of wood I had never seen before and four big windows taking up almost the whole of two walls, it was bright and airy.

The fireplace, too, was a handsome one with the Morley arms emblazoned on it and a little inglenook with a cushioned seat where one could sit before getting into bed. It also had a small dressing-room off it hidden behind a curtain to match the others which draped the windows.

"It's a lovely room," I said, standing in the middle of the thickly carpeted floor and looking around me with delight.

"So it is," she agreed. "Mrs. Morley can

say what she likes about Clifton Manor, but there aren't so many gentlemen's residences as handsome as it, that's certain sure. Even if it doesn't have any of this new-fangled lighting."

I laughed.

"Mrs. Morley would like to be up-to-date, I suppose?"

"Aye, and Mr. Philip, too, but Master would never agree. He said he didn't want his beautiful woodwork knocked about and a big noisy old engine pounding away and breaking down just when you needed light most."

"I'm glad he didn't. The lamps and candles are in keeping," I said fervently. "It would have been very costly, too."

"That wouldn't have worried the master. He was free enough with his money when he was sure it would be spent right. Whatever they two might say," she added, under her breath.

I did not ask her what she meant because I was thinking of my Grandfather and wishing I had known him. The more I heard about him the more sure I became that I could have loved him, even though he had turned Papa out of the Manor for marrying against his wishes.

That had been a shocking thing to do, of course, yet even while I acknowledged it I was remembering what Papa had been like. In his own way he had been every bit as autocratic as Grandfather and as unforgiving. Perhaps if Papa had written to Grandfather after a while and extended the olive branch, maybe when I was born, they might have been reconciled.

Perhaps if the son they had always hoped for had come, he might have done so. It was certain Grandfather could do nothing because he had no idea where his son had gone to or whether he was alive or dead. I only felt sure that he had regretted his impulsive action many times over the years.

"There," Mrs. Ramsden said with satisfaction, getting up from her knees after tidying the hearth. "Everything's done and the bed's well aired. Your Grandfather'd be glad if he knew you were in his old room, Miss Rachel."

"I think he is glad," I said quietly. "There's something—a welcoming feeling about it. And I like having that picture there."

She looked at it complacently.

"Mr. Philip was all for taking it down and putting it in the attics but I said no. It's been there since master had the likeness taken of his first wife, your Grandmama, my dear, and that's where I said it must be left until you decided whether you wanted it taken down or not."

"I don't. It's one of the things that makes me feel—oh, safe and wanted. I'm being stupid, aren't I, talking like this. As if everybody here hasn't been welcoming and kind to me."

"That's as maybe. Now, I must go and see what those girls are doing downstairs."

When I was alone I sat on the inglenook seat, looking back over the past few days, hardly able to believe so much could have happened in such a short time. My whole life had altered. From being poor and lonely with nowhere to go and without any prospects, I was the owner of a manor house and estate, and a big farm. I had money to spend, lovely new clothes, new friends, a place in the world again.

And, most wonderful of all, I had met

the man who before had only existed in my dreams, and had found him as ready to love me as I loved him. I had nothing left to wish for except to be sorry that none of this happened while my parents were alive to enjoy it with me.

I leaned back against the inglenook seat, happy because I was now in the room which in some way seemed still to be imbued with the presence of the Grandfather I had never known. Yet I did not deserve such happiness for my reasons for agreeing to this move had not been the right ones. I had said I would come, not because I wanted to but because Philip and his mother desired it.

An ignoble reason, I told myself guiltily, though surely it would be forgiven me. Because it was very necessary for me to gain Thea Morley's approbation and affection so that she would accept me more readily as her son's wife, when we were at last able to share our secret with her.

Yet even though I was so happy in my new room, I was still not brave enough to sleep in it without shooting the bolts with which the door was furnished. That was something I would do, I told myself as a tingle of excitement coursed through my body, until the night Philip closed our bedroom door and shut out the rest of the world from what would be our most utter and complete happiness.

When I announced that I had moved into Grandfather's room Philip and his mother said how pleased they were. Jason did not speak, only looking at me out of eyes almost hidden by his frowning brows so that I could not see their expression. But I did not care what he thought. I was only glad to know that I had pleased my dear Philip and done as he wished.

Not that he was in spirits. He was not his usual gay self at all, and I suspected that he was fretting because he was still dependent on Clifton Manor. One day, I told myself, I would be able to reassure him and bring back the brightness to his eyes and the gaiety to his bearing.

It was on the evening of the Sunday which was Meg's "day" off that a letter was delivered by hand for Philip and after he had read it his spirits seemed to become even more despondent. And mine matched them because for me the evening was proving a bitter disappointment, perhaps because I had expected too much from it.

When I had joined Philip and Thea he had told me Jason would not be coming in as he was spending the night at his own place and I had leaped to the conclusion that he was going to seize this splendid opportunity to tell his mother our wonderful news. But as time went on and he did not do so, I began to feel very low indeed.

Perhaps it was because of this despondency that when Philip folded the letter and thrust it into his pocket with a queer half-smile on his lips, it seemed to me that the whole atmosphere altered with its advent, and I shivered as if a blast of ice cold air had struck me.

"What news, my son?"

Thea's voice aroused me from the strange sensation which had visited me and I sat up straight, striving to thrust it from me.

"Nothing of any moment. It is as we suspected," Philip answered enigmatically.

She opened her blue eyes very wide, a movement which altered the whole expression of her face, making it look alive and, in some strange way, rather terrifying because it was so different from her normal languidly disinterested air.

"I see," she said at last, and thereafter no further mention was made of the letter.

Yet I had the strongest impression that its coming was very important to them both and marked a definite milestone in their lives. Later, looking back, I knew that for me it signified the end of a period of comparative peace and the beginning of an intensity of fear which stayed with me until the climax came at last.

It was not long after receiving the letter that Philip said with concern:

"You're in pain, Thea. Why didn't you tell me?"

"I'm so tired of being a nuisance to you, Philip. I am always ruining your pleasures and giving you trouble and worry."

"What nonsense! You know I enjoy caring for you. Is your back hurting very badly, dearest?"

"Yes, I'm afraid so."

"Then I'll take you upstairs to Anna. She will give you your cordial. You're very naughty to lie and suffer like this."

He bent and lifted her gently, and she smiled into his face.

"Thank you, Philip." Then she looked over to me. "I am sorry to break up your evening, Rachel, but I promise I'll send him back as soon as I can."

I stammered out some reply, and watched until they went through the door leading to Thea's apartments. Then I settled down to wait for Philip's return, feeling excitement beginning to burn through me at the prospect of being alone with him for the first time since he had held me in his arms. If only nobody came to spoil everything.

I knew Jason would not because Philip had said he was not coming back that night, but if Meg came in from her time off, then she would disturb us by bringing in the tea tray. I crossed my fingers, hoping that this might be one of the times she would come back late, risking Mrs. Ramsden's displeasure, because even half an hour alone with my love was very precious to me.

I was so lost in my dreams of what might happen that I took little heed of the clock and it was a while before I realized with a sense of shock that Philip had been gone for a long time. I watched the hour tick inexorably on, not allowing myself to believe that he did not intend to come, but feeling a cold surge of disappointment slowly creeping over me.

It was at the moment when my hopes had reached their lowest ebb that the door leading to the kitchen premises was thrown open and Mrs. Ramsden came in, almost running in her haste.

"Oh, Miss Rachel, can you come? Something terrible's happened."

I jumped up and ran to meet her.

"What is it?"

"It's Meg. Eddie's just brought her in. She's moaning and crying and wringing her hands something shocking. I can't do anything with her."

I took her arm without a word and hurried with her to the kitchen, though I could not forbear one last look in case Philip might be coming at last. But there was no sign of him and when we reached the kitchen every other thought was banished from my mind.

Because it was a scene of real confusion. Meg was crouched on the floor near the fire, shivering and sobbing, her dress muddied and marked with grass stains, her pretty face red and swollen with the tears she had shed. A young man whom I took to be Eddie was standing over her saying helplessly over and over again:

"Nay, lass. Nay, Meg." But not otherwise contributing anything useful to the scene.

I knelt down beside her and put my arm around her, saying:

"Meg, what's happened? Stop crying and tell us. Come, now, behave yourself."

But she only shuddered and cried the louder.

"Eh, it's no use talking to her. I've tried and so has Eddie," the housekeeper said, looking as if she herself would burst into tears at any moment.

I hesitated, wondering what was the right thing to do, knowing that until we could bring Meg to her senses and find out what had happened to her, we were not going to make any progress. But how to do that? Then I remembered a similar scene when I had first gone to work in the sewing factory.

One of the girls, about my own age, had

been sent to the store room for something, I could not remember what now, and as she had picked it up a big rat had leaped out at her and sunk its teeth into her hand. She had been so terrified that she had done nothing but scream and scream until we all rushed to her. By then the rat had gone and she was not able to tell us what had happened, until the forewoman filled a bucket with cold water and flung it over her.

Now, as Meg writhed on the floor, becoming more and more hysterical every minute, I knew what I had to do. I went into the scullery and, not being able to find a bucket readily, filled a bowl with cold water and, bringing it into the kitchen, threw the contents deliberately into Meg's face.

She screamed once, then her sobs turned into gasps as she choked over the water she had swallowed, but it worked. She sat up, dashing it from her eyes which had lost that strange glitter and were looking up at us as if she was seeing us for the first time.

"Oh, Miss Rachel!" she quavered. "How did I get here?"

"Eddie brought you," I said briskly, making my voice as unsympathetic as I could, feeling that the more matter-of-fact I sounded the better it would be. "Make some tea, will you, Mrs. Ramsden, but first go and get my new dressing-gown and we'll wrap Meg in it when we've dried her off a bit."

I went back into the scullery and caught up a towel, but when I began to dry Meg's face and hair she grasped my hand urgently.

"Oh, Miss, I saw it, plain as plain. It came straight out of the trees right at me. It was awful! It had no head and its hands were—were clawing at me!"

Her voice was rising again and I took her hands firmly in mine, saying sharply:

"Never mind now. You can tell us when you've had your tea. Come, get up and sit on the settle with Eddie. Do as I tell you."

She responded at once to the authority in my voice and began to struggle to her feet. Eddie came forward and helped her, taking her to the settle beside the fire and sitting down beside her, keeping her hand in his. Mrs. Ramsden came in then and shooed him away while she took off Meg's wet dress, ruined now by the water as well as mud and grass stains, and put my wrapper on her.

"Now, Eddie, you come back here while I make the tea," she said and added to me, "I took the liberty of going into Mr. Jason's rooms and taking the brandy he keeps there. He won't object when I tell him why, and they could both do with a dram."

"That was wise of you. Did you see anybody around? Mr. Philip or—?"

"No, not a soul, Miss Rachel. I wish Mr. Jason was here. He'd know what was best to do."

"We'll manage all right without him," I said quickly, though in spite of my denial, I was aware of something inside myself which agreed with the housekeeper. Because whatever I might think of his high-handed and arrogant ways, I had to admit he was a man who could be relied on in an emergency and part of my reaction was due to the knowledge that I had somehow come to depend on him far more than I should have done.

"Aye, maybe," Mrs. Ramsden said.

"Here's your tea. Would you like a drop of brandy in it?"

"No, thank you." I looked over to Meg and Eddie who were beginning to respond to the normalcy of the scene and to the brandy with which their tea had been liberally laced. "Are you able to tell us what happened, Meg? Without getting upset again."

"Yes, Miss. It was the white lady. I saw her only she didn't have no head. She came out of the trees right at me, clawing at me. Oh, it was horrible and I couldn't move a step. Then I got my legs back and I turned to run. Only I tripped and fell down." Her hand shook so much that Eddie had to take the cup from her. "I thought it was my end and I put my arms over my head. Then I heard Eddie shouting and I don't remember any more."

"Did you see anything, Eddie?" I asked.

"No. I heard Meg scream, eh, it were a terrible sound that, and I rushed back. When I saw you lying there, right close to that old pit, I thought you was dead, that I did."

200

"But you must have seen her, Eddie," Meg said, grasping his hand tightly.

"Nay, lass. I saw nothing but you. You must have dreamed it. I'm not surprised, neither. You and the missus done nothing all evening but talk about gypsies and ghosts. It's no wonder you were frightened half out of your wits."

"But I did see it," she said obstinately. "I did."

Her voice was rising again and I said quickly:

"All right, Meg. You'll feel better about it after you've had a night's sleep."

"I'll never be able to sleep again!"

"Yes, you will. Mrs. Ramsden will make up the day bed in my room for you and you can stay there tonight. I'll take care of you."

"Eddie—" she said, still clinging to him.

"Eddie must go back to the farm. They'll be wondering what's become of him. We'll take care of her," I added to him. "You can come tomorrow if you can be spared to see her, and I think you'll find she's better. Now, Meg, say good-night to Eddie."

She did as I bid her and he patted her awkwardly.

"Take care, lass, and do what Miss Rachel says."

When he had gone we took her upstairs and after she was safely tucked in, Mrs. Ramsden gave her a posset she had made.

"There!" she said. "That'll make you sleep like a babby all night. Will you be all right, Miss Rachel?"

"Yes. And thank you."

The housekeeper was right. Before I was in bed Meg was already deeply asleep, most of the strain gone from her face. But I was not so fortunate. I lay for a long time, glad of the light from my bedside lamp which I had turned half down, thinking over what we had been told.

Was it true, or was Eddie's theory that she had allowed the idea of the white lady to take too vivid a hold on her imagination the correct one? Yet I would have said she was a fairly phlegmatic girl, not given to wild imaginings.

Then I remembered what Eddie had said. She had been lying near the edge of the pit when he found her. What would have happened if she had not tripped, I thought with a shudder. Would she, in her blind fear of this thing she had thought was following her, have gone hurtling over the edge as my Grandfather and his horse had? Had they, too, seen the headless woman in white?

I sat up quickly, appalled by that thought, and turned up the lamp, looking across at Meg to make sure she was indeed sleeping quietly instead of lying at the bottom of that still mere in the dark pit. Suppose she had not screamed or Eddie had not heard her? Would she have been left lying unconscious at the edge or—?

I moved restlessly, trying to shut out the terrifying thoughts and pictures which were tormenting me. But I could not and it was not until tired nature at last had its way that I fell into a shallow sleep.

I was hardly asleep a minute, or so it seemed, when I was wide awake again, holding my breath, listening for the sound that had disturbed me but which I could not identify. Then I heard it again. A quiet tap on the door.

I was out of bed in a moment, huddling my wrapper around me. Then I padded over to the door on bare feet to stand silently beside it, listening and waiting for I knew not what. I only knew I was afraid to speak, afraid to open the door in case I, too, saw the headless woman who had so terrified Meg.

Then the tap came again and a voice whispered:

"Rachel! Are you awake?"

It was Philip and with great relief I pulled back the bolts and opened the door.

"Philip! Is anything wrong? Your mother?"

"Yes. She isn't at all well and Anna wants hot milk to help her to settle. I said I'd get it but there's no one in the kitchen."

"It's so late."

"I realize that now, so I went up to Meg's room to ask her to come down. Rachel, she isn't there. Where can she be? It's almost midnight."

I laughed softly.

"Were you worried about her? How like you to care. She's quite safe and sleeping soundly. She had a bad fright tonight and was afraid to stay by herself, so I've got her here in my room."

I saw an expression cross his face which I could not interpret, then he was smiling.

"What a relief! I thought I would probably have to turn out to search for her and I wasn't looking forward to that. Can you wake her, Rachel? I must have some hot milk."

"I don't think so. Mrs. Ramsden made her a posset and she's in a really deep sleep. I'll—"

I broke off as I heard a door opening and saw Jason standing looking at us, fully dressed as was Philip. He came towards us at his usual quick pace.

"What's wrong," he asked sharply.

I put my fingers to my lips.

"Hush. Meg's asleep in my room. She's had rather a terrifying experience tonight and I don't want her disturbed. I was just going down to the kitchen with Philip to heat some milk for his mother."

"Can't Anna get it?"

"She can't leave Thea. Come along, Philip."

"No need to trouble Rachel," Jason said in his usual peremptory way. "I know where the milk is kept and I'm capable of heating some, even if you're not, Philip.

Go back to bed or you'll be contracting a chill or rheumatic fever, standing there with bare feet," he added to me.

I could see the frown marring Philip's brow and felt a thrill of pleasure at the sight, because it must mean that, like me, he was annoyed at Jason's interference which had put an end to our few moments together.

"If you don't mind, Philip," I said, determined to go with him if he wanted me to, in spite of Jason and in spite of the fact that my feet were already numb from the cold draught which swept along the passage.

"Of course I don't," he said at once. "It was selfish of me to expect it of you at this time of night, but I'm very worried about Thea."

"Goodnight then, Rachel," Jason said. "I hope the rest of the night will be undisturbed."

I watched them walk along the passage together, then went back into the room, bolting the door before climbing into bed. It was as I lay down that I remembered! Philip had said Jason was not coming back to Clifton Manor that night, yet he had been there, had looked in fact as if he had only recently arrived. He must have changed his mind, I thought, and was glad he had done so. It was a relief to know that both he and Philip were near if I needed them.

I wrapped my cold feet in the bottom of my long nightgown, huddling under the covers, expecting to lie awake until I was warm again. But I was wrong.

I must have fallen asleep almost at once, my last conscious thought being the comforting one that Philip had not deliberately stayed away from me. He had not come back because he could not leave his mother when she was so ill. And I honoured him for that.

11

MEG woke before me next morning. She was almost dressed when I opened my eyes and seemed her usual cheerful self.

"Eh, I don't know what you must be thinking of me, Miss Rachel," she said when she realized I had wakened. "Carrying on like I did and putting you all about. It'd be no wonder if you turned me off."

"As if I would, Meg. Something frightened you badly, that I'm sure of, and I was only too happy to have you with me last night."

She stood where she was, obviously thinking hard.

"I remember Eddie saying I must have imagined it, Miss Rachel, and maybe he was right." Then an expression of fear clouded her eyes and she said, "Whatever it was I was terrified. That's my only excuse."

"Don't think about it any more." I

208

hesitated, wanting to warn her to take care in future, without frightening her again, knowing that I would feel happier if she did not wander away from the house by herself. Then I thought of a way to do it. "I see what it is, Meg. You'll have to take care of me and I of you. Neither of us must move a step without the other outside this house, because we're not to be trusted on our own."

She laughed at that, but agreed, then went to the door to go up to her attic bedroom to finish dressing, tugging at the door but failing to open it.

"You'll have to undo the bolts first," I said. "I locked us in last night."

"Just as well, too, though it's a wonder you weren't afraid to be locked in the same room with somebody as foolish as me. I'll bring your breakfast and hot water as soon as I can, Miss Rachel."

I lay back against the pillow when she had gone, frowning over what she had said. She seemed to have accepted that she had imagined the whole thing, yet I was not convinced. I could see her now lying on the kitchen floor, almost crazed with terror. She had believed then that she had seen a ghost.

Now in the light of day she was ashamed of her fears, but I had the feeling that as evening approached they might overcome her again. Perhaps if I were to persuade her to come with me to the old pit so that she could see for herself there was nothing there, it might help. And at the same time I could perhaps satisfy myself that there was no evidence of an attacker, whether supernatural or not. That thought pulled me up with a jolt. It was the first intimation I had had that my mind was moving in the direction of a living person who might have frightened Meg for her own reasons and then been afraid of the reaction she had provoked. Might it not have been the gypsy, underlining her own predictions in this way to give them credence? If it was, then somewhere she might have left a sign of some kind and I determined to look for it.

It was at that point that there came a knock at the door and Jason strode in already dressed in his many caped riding coat and carrying his hat and crop.

"What happened to Meg last night?" he asked in his usual peremptory fashion.

I pulled the bedclothes around my shoulders and felt the colour rise in my cheeks.

"You oughtn't to come in here—"

"Don't be childish, Rachel. You're covered far more modestly by your nightwear than many women are at a dinner party. Forget about yourself and tell me about Meg."

I did as he asked although I would have preferred to order him out of my room instead of weakly allowing him to sit on the bottom of my bed while he listened to what I had to say. Yet it was in truth a relief to tell him because deep down inside I was almost as afraid as Meg had been last night and wanted some reassurance that she had in fact been frightened by shadows and her own imagination.

"She thought she actually saw a headless woman clad in white," he said incredulously when I had finished my tale.

"Yes, and she really believed it. She was in a frantic state, but this morning she feels she was mistaken."

He looked at me penetratingly, hearing the doubt in my voice.

"But you don't think she was?"

"I don't know. I was wondering if perhaps it was the gypsy—"

"Then you needn't. I know the gypsies. They are friendly people who wouldn't harm Meg or anyone else."

"Then I can only think—Jason, it happened at the place where Grandfather was killed. Meg tried to run away from this—whatever it was. If she hadn't tripped she would have fallen down the pit, like he did. Suppose he saw this ghost and that's why—"

"It would be better if you controlled your imagination, Rachel," he said curtly. "I'll believe in a headless woman when I see her and not before. What time did Meg come in?"

I was surprised by his question and did not attempt to hide it.

"It was about quarter past nine when Mrs. Ramsden came for me. Why? What difference does it make?"

He did not answer my questions but asked me another one.

"Who was with you?"

212

"Nobody. I was alone and had been for some time. You see, Thea's back was paining her, so Philip took her to her room. He—She said he'd come back but he didn't."

"What time was this?"

"Soon after we had finished supper. About a quarter past eight."

"So you were on your own for an hour?"

"Yes. Jason, do you think—"

"I don't think anything, and it would be better if you didn't either." Then he got up and came to me, laying his hand for a moment against my cheek. "You're a good girl, Rachel. Mrs. Ramsden told me how well you coped with Meg's hysterics. I am proud of you."

I was so overcome by his words and action that at first I could not speak. When I did, to my annoyance all I could say was:

"I'm afraid we drank most of your brandy."

He smiled.

"It was in a good cause. Rachel, will you promise me something?"

"If I can," I said cautiously.

"You can. Don't speak of this to

anyone, anyone at all. And that includes Thea and Philip."

I stared at him, trying to read the meaning behind his words.

"But I've already told Philip that Meg had a bad fright."

"That was all?"

"Yes, but he's bound to ask me about it."

"I don't think he will."

"Certainly he will. He was very concerned about Meg. When she wasn't in her room—"

"He looked for her there?"

"Yes, then he came to me. He was very surprised to find she was asleep on my day bed."

"So I should imagine," he said with a peculiar intonation. "Well, if he does ask you, then you'll have to tell him. All I am asking is that you don't volunteer the story. After all, it doesn't put Meg in a very good light and might lead to her dismissal."

"It won't because I shan't let it," I said militantly. "But I see what you mean and I promise I'll do as you ask."

"Thank you."

He turned towards the door and I, impelled by an urgency for which I could not account, said quickly:

"Are you going to the mill?"

"Yes. As usual."

"Will you return tonight?"

He looked at me thoughtfully.

"Why?"

"I don't know. I just wondered. Philip said you were going to stay in your house beside the works last night, and as you didn't, I wondered if perhaps tonight—"

"I shall be in tonight," he said deliberately, "but tomorrow evening I have an appointment with Mr. Lacey and he has asked me to stay overnight with him. Don't you wish me to do that?"

I coloured at his tone.

"What you do is of no interest to me!" I snapped.

"Then there is no reason for me to come back," he answered.

"None at all!" Then a thought occurred to me and I said anxiously, "Are you going to discuss my business?"

"Perhaps, but Lacey is my solicitor, too, and I have some legal matters connected with the mill that I wish to talk to him about."

"Oh. I see."

I was unable to disguise my disappointment and he frowned at me.

"Rachel, don't be too trusting. You may be—"

I waited but when he said no more, I asked:

"Why do you say that?"

"No reason. Forget it. I see it's no use —Goodbye."

He turned on the words and went quickly out of the room. I lay for a long time after he left me wishing I could understand him. What a mixture he was! Sometimes so kind and thoughtful. At others scornful and dictatorial, giving me half warnings which he could not or would not explain.

What could he mean by telling me not to be so trusting, by warning me not to speak about Meg's adventure? There was no sense in asking me to give that promise, especially as I knew Philip was sure to want to know all about it. And if by any chance he did not, then it was still my duty to tell him. He was the man I hoped to marry one day and I ought not to have any secrets from him. Of course Jason could not know that and I could not tell him, because of the promise I had made to my dearest Philip.

I felt a warm glow pulse through me as I looked into the future when he would be with me for always as my husband, and forgot about Meg and Jason and his strange request, remembering only the happiness which would be mine one day soon.

When Meg brought me my breakfast she told me it was raining and I was disappointed. I would not be able to go with her to the old pit and possibly before I could do so, all trace of any human being would be gone, washed away by the downpour. From my own recollection of the place, it would soon become a quagmire which would not readily dry out again.

The rain continued all day and I stayed quietly in the house. But it was an uneasy quiet. Somehow the lowering skies, the sound of the rain which as the day advanced was flung against the windows by a rising wind which howled around the Manor like a live thing, seemed both menacing and terrifying. I was glad when Meg went round early lighting the lamps and pulling the curtains across the streaming windows.

"That's better, Miss Rachel," she said as she made up the fire and swept the hearth. "Makes it a deal cosier, shutting out that wind and rain."

"Yes," I said but I did not feel any better, perhaps because I had been too much alone all day, hardly speaking to anybody except Mrs. Ramsden and Meg.

I had knocked on the door of Thea's apartments earlier to ask how she was feeling and Anna, her maid, had said curtly in reply to my enquiry that she was no better and Mr. Philip had ridden off to see her doctor and get the drugs which she needed when these attacks came. So I had not even the comfort of Philip's presence during the whole of that dreary day.

Meg brought the tea in and went away quickly as she had other duties to perform, and I was feeling very sorry for myself and quite deserted when Jason came striding into the hall from the side passage.

"Tea," he said. "Good. I'll have a cup before I go and change."

I was absurdly pleased to see him and minister to him, to such straits was I reduced.

"Have you ridden through all this? You must be soaked."

"I had my waterproofs on, so I'm not too wet. I am cold, though," he added and took up his usual stance at the side of the roaring fire, his tea cup in his hand.

He looked at me over the rim, his eyes penetratingly alive, and I leaned back in my chair so that my face was in shadow, afraid that his keen gaze would read all my most private thoughts.

"What is worrying you?" he asked sharply.

"Nothing. It's just that I've been alone all day and—"

I stopped, feeling ashamed of my stupidity, of the deep depression which filled me. It had receded now that he had come, for whatever my private opinion of him might be, I had to admit that by his mere presence he could dissipate my troubles and fears.

He put down his cup and came closer to me.

"What is it, Rachel. Won't you tell me?"

He took my hand in his, holding it tightly and I felt the warmth from it seeping through me and bringing me comfort.

"It's nothing. I'm just being stupid. I expect it's the weather. I don't like a howling wind. It frightens me. I'm a coward, I suppose."

His fingers tightened on mine and he said so gently that I could hardly believe it was the Jason I knew talking:

"You're not a coward, Rachel. You're a very brave girl. Too brave for your own good, sometimes. I wish—"

I waited a moment, then said shyly, surprised at the pleasure which thrilled through me at his touch and his praise, "What do you wish?"

He let go of my hand abruptly and moved back to the fireplace, and I felt bereft, as if I had lost something dear to me.

"Nothing. It's no use—I must go and change. I'll see you later, Rachel."

I watched him run up the stairs, my mind in a turmoil. I did not understand him in the least. He had been so different, not a bit his usual calm and confident self, yet when I looked back over our conversation, I could find nothing to explain the change I thought I saw in him. So in the end I came to the conclusion that I was wrong. That my own over-active imagination had tricked me into seeing something that was not really present.

Philip had still not come in when I went up to change for the evening and his continued absence made me feel depressed again. When I was ready I went downstairs, hoping he might have arrived, but only Jason was there, reading a paper which he put down when he saw me.

"Mrs. Ramsden says there will only be you and I for supper tonight. Thea is still very unwell and Philip came in only to bring her medicine and change before going out again."

"Philip has gone out again?"

"Yes. Why? Shouldn't he have done?"

I felt my face burn under his surprised gaze and was afraid I had given myself away. Perhaps betrayed the secret Philip had asked me to keep. So I shrugged and said as casually as I could:

"It's nothing to me what he does. I only thought it strange he should go out on such a dreadful night."

He laughed.

"Ah, but we men are strange indeed. We never mind the weather when there's a lovely lady waiting for us at the end of our journey."

I was so surprised to hear Jason speak so gaily that I almost missed the import of what he had said.

"You think that is true of Philip?" I asked, in what I hoped was an equally gay tone.

"Yes. I expect Miss Ainsworth has summoned him to take dinner and spend the evening with them."

"Miss Ainsworth? Surely not," I was betrayed into saying.

He raised his eyebrows.

"Why not? Philip has always had a tendre in that direction."

"But not—" I began, then recollected in time to stop myself from telling Jason that Philip loved me and not this other girl.

"Not what?"

"Oh, nothing. Naturally he can come

222

and go as he likes in this house," I said quickly, and was glad that Mrs. Ramsden came in then to tell us supper was ready to be served, even though I was not looking forward to eating alone with Jason. It would probably be a dull and silent meal.

But I had misjudged him, because he was a most entertaining and comfortable companion. He talked about everything except what had happened to me since the night Mama had died, and I laughed more than I had done for a very long time.

Afterwards, when we parted later that night, I remembered this with surprise. Never before had it occurred to me that although I was so comfortable here, with no more money worries and with clothes such as I had never worn before in my life, I had not laughed spontaneously. I had, in fact, found nothing at all to laugh at. Which was strange, because Mama and I had found lots to laugh at and enjoy, even though we had been so poor.

Oh, I had smiled and been happy when Mrs. Ramsden or Meg had been with me and when Philip had told me he loved me. But these were isolated happenings and until that night when Jason and I were alone together, there had been no lightness, and very little gaiety or laughter.

And I was grateful to him because he had lifted the heavy pall of depression which had obsessed me all that day, so that as I prepared for bed I felt quite lighthearted. Though not light-hearted enough to forget to bolt the bedroom door, nor to leave my lamp burning low.

Yet as I settled down in the big bed I had the strange feeling that somebody somewhere was looking after me and safeguarding me, and I wondered if it was Mama and Papa, or perhaps Grandfather who was watching over me.

12

IT continued to rain all the next day
so that the garden looked sodden and
dreary and the surrounding hills were
hidden in a thick mist. Again I spent the
day alone although I had the evening to
look forward to when Philip would be
home.

"I have to go out, Rachel," he said
when I came upon him as he was about to
leave the house, "but I'll be back in time
for supper."

"Will your mother be well enough to get
up for it?"

"Alas, no. Anna thinks she is somewhat
improved but she won't be up for some
days yet."

"Then we'll be alone, you and I," I said
eagerly. "Jason is dining with Mr. Lacey
and will stay the night there."

"Is he?" He smiled then and put his
hand under my chin, lifting my face up to
his. "Then that will give me something to
look forward to while I am doing all my

dreary business." And he bent and brushed my lips with his.

That caress and his promise kept me happy all day and I spent more time than usual on my toilet so that I would look my best for Philip. But it was all wasted. For when Philip came he could not stay.

"Rachel, forgive me, but I must go back to Thea. She has been very low all day and has implored me to stay with her, so I must."

"Oh, Philip," I said, trying to blink back the tears of disappointment that filled my eyes.

"I am disappointed too, my love, but you wouldn't want me to desert her when she needs me so much. And it isn't often she allows herself to give way to melancholy, even though she has cause enough to."

I swallowed hard.

"No, of course you must go to her. I wouldn't want you to do anything else."

He pressed my hand in both of his.

"I knew you would say that. Forgive me, Rachel."

"There's nothing to forgive," I said and

was almost reduced to tears again when he lifted my hand to his lips.

I had my supper in solitary state in the dining-room. I would have liked to have eaten in the kitchen with Mrs. Ramsden and Meg but I did not suggest it, knowing that they would not have refused but would have felt inhibited by my presence.

I sat in front of the fire afterwards reading, hoping against hope that Philip might come and spend a little time with me, perhaps if his mother fell asleep but the minutes ticked away and he did not come.

Meg brought the tea tray early to me and I decided that when I had drunk my tea I would go to bed. There seemed little else to do. I was just on the point of retiring when Meg came back carrying a small silver tray holding a glass of wine.

"Mr. Philip sent you this," she said. "You're to drink it at half-past nine exactly, and he's going to drink one at the same time. He says you know what the toast is to be."

I did not know but I could guess, and I was happy that Philip had thought of this

way of bidding me goodnight and re-
minding me of our secret.

There was only a few minutes to wait
and when the time came I lifted up my
glass and said, quietly:

"To you, my dearest Philip, and to our
future together. With all my love."

I took a sip of the wine and shuddered
because it was so bitter. It was even worse
than the sherry Jason had given me on the
first night I arrived at Clifton Manor and
which I had steadfastly refused ever since.
I tried to take another sip, but my stomach
revolted against it and I had to use my
handkerchief to clear my mouth.

"I'm sorry, Philip," I said, "I cannot
drink to you, but you have all my love and
good wishes. We don't need wine to seal
that."

But I did not want him to come through
later on his way to bed and find an almost
full glass of wine, so I carefully poured the
remains behind the fire, then put the glass
down on the table, empty.

When I got to my bedroom I had to
hurry into the dressing-room where I was
sick again into the flowered wash bowl,

but after that my stomach seemed to settle itself and I slowly prepared for bed.

I was asleep almost as soon as my head touched the pillow, to awake suddenly and completely I could not tell how much later to complete darkness.

I lay without moving for a moment before I realized that my lamp had gone out, and was just about to sit up and grope for the matches which I always kept beside it when I heard a sound, a sharp distinct click as if a latch had been released, and froze in my bed, every faculty on the stretch. There was somebody in the room with me.

I could not see them nor could I hear them, yet every nerve in my body told me that I was no longer alone. Yet who could have got in? I had securely bolted the door before getting into bed, yet I was sure that the sound I had heard was a door being closed carefully.

Some instinct prevented me from holding my breath as I wanted to, told me to go on breathing as if I was still asleep, and through the darkness and the sound of my own even breathing I strained eyes and ears. And then I heard it. A faint sound as if a shoe had brushed against something as the wearer moved carefully over the thick carpet, a slight sound as if somebody's breath had caught in his throat.

I could hear my heart beating unevenly in my breast as I strained my eyes to see, watching the faint light from the dying fire in case a shadow passed across it. If only my lamp was alight. Why had it gone out this night when it had remained alight every other night?

I could feel my mouth drying up with fear, fear that made me afraid to move, afraid to make any sound in case the intruder whose presence I sensed would realize that I was awake. For some queer inner sense of self-preservation warned me that my only hope lay in the fact that the person, whoever it was, thought I still slept. That way I might remain in control of the situation.

It was at that moment that I saw the faint shadow in the dying firelight and sensed rather than saw something descending on me. I heaved myself to one side and screamed at the full stretch of my lungs, a scream which was cut off abruptly as a thick suffocating softness was pressed over my face, preventing me from breathing.

I struggled, trying to push the thing away, but it was held down relentlessly by strong hands. Then as I felt my senses begin to swim I heard Jason's voice calling:

"Rachel, let me in. What's the matter?"

As if the sound of his voice had shocked my assailant, the pressure on my face relaxed and with a last despairing effort I managed to push off the suffocating thing and croaked as loudly as I could:

"Jason, quick, quick."

Then it came down again but this time my hands were under it, holding it off so that there was a space over my mouth, and at the same moment the room began to shake under Jason's onslaught on the bolted door.

Suddenly, almost without realizing it, I was free. The grip on the thing over my face was relaxed and I pushed it off, gulping in the air which my lungs had been denied, almost retching as I did so.

The door was still shuddering under the

impact of Jason's body and I forced myself to get out of bed and stagger over to it.

"Wait! I'm here," I said but could not know whether he had heard me because of the noise he was making.

I stooped and released the bottom bolt with shaking fingers, and the assault on the door ceased as if he had realized what I was doing. Then I pushed back the top one and leaned against the door, without the strength to stand aside. But he must have guessed I was there because he opened the door very slowly and edged his way in, taking me in his arms and holding me close to him for a few moments.

"Rachel," he said at last. "What's happened? Why did you scream?"

But I could not reply. I only clung to him more closely, the deep sobs I could no longer control shuddering through me, and without saying any more he picked me up in his arms and carried me to the bed. He laid me on it then struck a match and tried to light the lamp but it would not light and with an impatient exclamation he went to the dressing-table and lit the candles on it.

I lay with closed eyes, trying to regain

control of myself, telling myself that everything was all right now Jason had come. Then I felt him lift me until my head was cradled against his shoulder and heard his voice saying, as decisively as ever:

"Drink this, Rachel. It will make you feel better."

I did as he said and the raw spirit caught at my throat and made me cough.

"Oh, what is it?"

"Brandy. Come, drink it up. It will do you good."

I did as he said, leaning against him, feeling safe and secure in the circle of his arm, and gradually I began to recover from the shock I had had.

Then Jason pushed back the hair from my forehead gently and said:

"Do you feel able to tell me what frightened you, Rachel?"

I nodded, still clutching his hands tightly.

"I'd been asleep but I woke suddenly. There was a noise, like a door closing and the lamp had gone out. I knew there was somebody there. Jason, he tried to smother me! Something came down on my face and I screamed. Then I couldn't breathe. I heard you at the door and the person—whoever it was, went away."

I was shuddering again at the end of my story and his grip tightened on me.

"It's over now," he said. "I'm here. I won't let anything hurt you. You're sure you weren't dreaming?"

"No, I wasn't. I was wide awake."

He laid me back against the pillow and made to stand up but I clutched him and said shakily:

"Don't go. Don't leave me, Jason."

"I'm not going. I want to look around, that's all." When he came back he stood beside me and said gravely:

"How many pillows do you use, Rachel?"

I stared at him.

"One."

"There's another one here. On the floor."

He bent and picked something up, holding it out to me.

"Where did it come from? I never have more than one."

"You're sure?"

"Of course I am," I cried, annoyance

because he seemed to disbelieve me helping me to regain my usual composure.

"Then someone else brought it in. Do you think—did it feel as though a pillow was held over your face?"

I was silent, trying to think back, to identify the thing which had been used, but I could not be sure.

"I don't know. It could have been. It was soft and cloying. But who was it and how did he get in?"

He frowned.

"I can only think of one way, but to my knowledge that was closed off long ago."

"What way?"

He did not answer but walked over to the wall beside the fireplace and began to press part of the carvings on it. At first nothing happened, then there was a distinct click.

"That's it!" I cried. "That's the sound I heard."

"You're sure?"

"Yes. The first click must have wakened me and then I heard a second one."

"The panel opening and shutting again."

I stared at him.

"What panel?"

He came and sat down on the bed.

"You know about the priest's hole and the passage from it?"

"Yes. Philip showed it to me but he said the passage had been closed."

"It had been but it looks as if it's been opened again."

"You mean—it leads up to this room?"

"Yes. It seems to have been secured from the other side so that we can't open it from here."

"You mean I locked myself into a room with a secret door in it? Why didn't you tell me about it? I'd never have moved into this room if I'd known."

"I don't blame you, but it was definitely closed off when your Grandfather was alive."

I was silent, not looking at him, my fingers moving restlessly against the quilt as I tried to assimilate what I had been told, feeling terror begin to rise within me.

"Then I can't stay in this room. He may come back. Jason, who could it have been? Who would want to kill me?"

He pulled me against him, holding me tightly.

"I don't know, Rachel, but believe me I intend to find out," he said grimly. "Look, suppose I push that big press against the panel. That will secure it and nobody will be able to get into the bedroom without removing it."

"You're sure there isn't another way in?"

"Quite sure. Please believe me, Rachel."

"All right," I said reluctantly, even though I could not think of a reasonable alternative to his suggestion. Because the one I would have liked to put in operation was out of the question. How could I ask Jason to stay with me for the rest of the night so that I would be safe? Already I knew he had been with me too long for the conventions, even though he had left the door open.

"It's a wonder nobody else came," I said suddenly, prompted by an association of ideas.

He nodded.

"Yes, isn't it. Very strange that Philip didn't hear you scream. His room is only a few doors away. Nearer than mine and I heard you very clearly."

"Perhaps he's still with his mother."

"With Thea? Why?"

"She's been very melancholy, you know, and begged him to stay with her. He didn't come in to supper."

"Were you all alone? Poor Rachel," he said with a smile.

I remembered something then.

"You came home, Jason. I thought you were going to stay with Mr. Lacey."

"I changed my mind."

"That was lucky for me," I said thankfully. "It was lucky for me, too, that you hadn't gone to bed."

"I hadn't been in long and was writing up some notes. Then I heard you call and came at once."

"Call?" I repeated.

"Yes. You screamed my name. Didn't you know?"

"No."

I could feel my face beginning to burn at the implication of what he had said, and he touched my head briefly and said:

"You'll have no more trouble tonight, Rachel. Now, I'll pull the press over."

When he had done that he smiled at me and held my hands for a brief minute.

"Goodnight, my dear. Bolt your door if you want to but you'll be quite safe. I'll be watching over you."

It was only by the exercise of a great deal of restraint that I prevented myself from begging him to stay with me until morning. Which was so forward of me that I was still blushing at the notion when I got back into bed after pushing in the bolts.

Not that I expected to sleep. I knew that if I did not lie awake all night I would only doze spasmodically, even though all the candles were burning. I had a great deal too much to think about to sleep.

Who would want to bring about my death? That was the truth I forced myself to face up to during the rest of that night. I had still no idea who had hit me the day I had fallen into the ha-ha, any more than I knew who was responsible for this night's terror.

I tossed restlessly in my bed, fear coursing through me as I admitted to myself that but for Jason, one or other of the attacks would have succeeded, but luckily he had been at hand both times to save me. I had so much to thank him for.

And in that moment I acknowledged that my first hasty assessment of him had been wrong. Because nobody could have been kinder to me than he had been since I had come to Clifton Manor, and that in the face of a dislike of him which I had never tried to hide.

But that was all over, and perhaps one day I would be able to tell him how much I regretted my behaviour to him.

13

IT was bright daylight when I awoke next morning aware that something had disturbed me without knowing what it was. Then it came again, a quiet tap on the door, and I sat up.

"Who is it?" I called.

"It's me. Meg."

I was just about to tell her to come in when I remembered I had bolted my door after Jason had left me. I got up and padded across the room to draw back the bolts and Meg came in, saying with an air of relief:

"You're awake at last, Miss Rachel. I've been up a few times and so has Mr. Philip, but we couldn't make you hear."

"Mr. Philip?"

"Yes. He wanted to see you and when you didn't answer his knock he got real worried. He'd have liked to break down the door but Mr. Jason wouldn't let him. He said you were all right and we had to let you wake natural like, because you'd had a bad nightmare and thought you'd heard somebody trying to get into your room through that old passage."

She looked from me to the press which Jason had moved and I said quickly:

"Yes, I did. I made a great deal of noise, too, and Mr. Jason heard me and came and woke me up. It made me feel very nervous, so he pulled the press in front of the passage entrance and told me to bolt my door as well."

I tried to speak calmly, but I could not help shuddering inwardly as I remembered what had really happened, though in the daylight it seemed unbelievable. Only the press in its new position convinced me I had not really dreamed it all. I had so much to be grateful to Jason for, even while I was irritated with him because he had kept Philip from me.

"You should have wakened me, Meg. What time is it?"

"It's gone eleven, Miss."

"Eleven! I must get up. Will you tell Mr. Philip I'll be down very soon, please."

"He's gone out, Miss Rachel."

"Oh. Did he say when he'd be back?"

"No. Him and Mr. Jason went off

together. Shall I fetch you your breakfast now?"

"Yes, please Meg."

I lay back in the bed, wondering what Philip had wanted me for and feeling disappointed because I had not seen him, and where he and Jason had gone. But Meg had come back with my breakfast before I had thought of a satisfactory answer to either of those questions.

When I had eaten I got up and dressed, finding my face a little sore and tender but otherwise feeling no ill-effects from the happenings in the night.

There was nobody about when I went downstairs. I had put on a mantle and tied a light scarf around my head, and after a moment's hesitation I walked out through the side door into the grounds for a breath of fresh air, meaning to stay near to the house. Then my eye was caught by a flash of colour in the small copse and I started impulsively towards it, sure that it was Philip's blue coat I had seen. But before I reached it I stopped, remembering my promise to Jason.

I had said I would not wander away from the house without Meg to accompany me and I knew I must not fail him now, no matter how much I wanted to see Philip. I peered into the clump of trees but could see that flash of blue no longer, then began reluctantly to walk back to the house.

As I reached it I was amply rewarded for my obedience. Philip came round the corner of the house, dressed in riding clothes, a whip in his hand.

"Philip!" I said happily. "At last. Oh, I am glad to see you."

I flung myself at him and felt his arm go round me and his lips brush my cheek lightly. Then he put me from him and stepped back.

"Careful, Rachel," he warned. "Someone might see us."

I looked at him, feeling quite deflated by his words and by the frown between his unsmiling eyes.

"I'm sure nobody will see us here. Anyway, one day soon everybody will be told."

"One day isn't now," he said, so sharply that I could hardly believe I was talking to the Philip I thought I knew.

"What's the matter? Meg said you were looking for me but now—"

He seemed to pull himself together and a smile lit up his face as he came closer to me.

"I'm sorry, my love. The fact is Jason told me what took place last night and I've been almost ill with worry ever since."

Suddenly I felt again the fear which had wracked me last night and I shuddered.

"It was awful, Philip. It was so lucky he was still up and heard me scream, otherwise I don't know what would have happened."

"You're sure there was someone there? You weren't dreaming?"

"Of course not. I can still feel that pressure on my face. Philip, it was terrifying."

I put out my hands to him and he held them gently, looking at me consideringly.

"You're sure Jason was outside the room while the other—whoever it was—was inside?"

"Yes. Why? What can you mean?"

"Well, he was supposed to stay with Mr. Lacey, wasn't he? What made him come back?"

"He changed his mind, which was lucky for me. Philip, he really was outside the door. He almost broke it down because I'd bolted it, top and bottom," I said earnestly. "It was he who frightened the intruder away. You must believe that."

"I do, if you say so, my love. Only I can't help wondering why you should be attacked. I ask myself who would benefit if anything happened to you and," he shrugged helplessly, "always the answer is Jason."

I was aware of a surge of angry denial which surprised me.

"That is ridiculous. Why, it is he who has saved me on two occasions!"

"Yes, that is true. He was there, on the spot, both times. Very fortuitous, you must agree."

I put my hands over my ears.

"No, I don't agree. I won't listen to you, Philip."

"Very well," he said repressively, moving a step away from me. "I am only thinking of your good, Rachel, but of course if you prefer to trust Jason before me—"

"That isn't true! It's you I love and trust. Only I feel sure you're wrong about him."

"Perhaps I am, but you cannot really blame me for thinking the worst. Especially when it is you who was in danger. I wish I had heard you calling."

I smiled at him, relieved and comforted by his words.

"I wish you had. It's a marvel you didn't. Jason said I made the devil's own noise."

"Those words do not sound well on your lips, Rachel. Don't let Thea hear you speak like that or I will never be able to tell her of our love."

I had the urge to inform him that if he was as narrow-minded as that perhaps it would be better if we made sure there was nothing to tell his mother. But I restrained myself, because it was very obvious that he was labouring under a considerable irritation of the nerves on my account. I should be glad of that and not add to it by anything I said.

"I'm sorry, love," I murmured contritely.

"It is all right. Naturally I would have preferred to be the one to look after you, especially as it meant Jason being in your

bedroom under such compromising circumstances."

"I understand," I said, but I did not
really because jealousy such as this was a
mystery to me. I should, I suppose, have
been glad he felt as he did, yet it brought
me no pleasure, only a feeling of irritation.
"Are you coming in?"

"No. I must go out again. When will
you be riding, Rachel?"

"Soon, I hope. Lizzie has almost
finished my habit and when she delivers
it, perhaps you will allow me to
accompany you. On a suitably quiet
horse," I added, with a smile.

"I shall look forward to that. Until later,
Rachel."

He bent and brushed my cheek with his
lips then walked towards the stables. I
watched until he was out of sight but he
did not turn round again. Then I went in
through the side door, my spirits sinking.
Apparently I was not yet to be forgiven
though I did not know for what, and as I
went up to my room I was conscious of a
stir of irritation at Philip's attitude.

Thea joined us for supper that evening,
but I did not think she looked at all well.

However, she received my expressions of concern with so patent a dislike of them that I said no more and we sat without talking until Jason came. He went straight to Thea's sofa, barely acknowledging my greeting.

"Thea, how are you? Philip tells me you've been in great pain."

"I have, but today I am better." All the animation had come back into her voice and face and I felt a twinge of annoyance at the difference with which she treated him. Of course, he was a very personable man, I thought, though years younger than her. But perhaps neither of them viewed that situation with the distaste it aroused in me. "I was so tired of being in my room that I risked joining you for supper. You never came to see me," she added reproachfully.

"I have been very busy and did not want to disturb you when perhaps you were sleeping. Philip told me how you went on. Where is he?"

"He has ridden to dearest Elaine with a letter from me. She, too, has not called on me for days. I do not know what I have done that all my friends desert me like this."

I thought she looked at me with an expression of malevolence and felt an icy shiver run down my spine. Yet how could that be? She was not aware that Philip and I loved each other and that Elaine would never be her daughter-in-law, though I wondered suddenly if perhaps she was becoming suspicious.

I sat quietly in my chair beside the fire, wishing Philip would come back though probably if he found Elaine in he would be asked to stay with her for a meal. The other two continued to talk in a low-voiced, confidential way, and I began to feel as though I was superfluous, and very lonely and neglected, not by Thea but by Jason. I had grown used to him taking care of me, paying me attention and tonight when he was not doing so, I felt quite upset.

Then Philip came running down the stairs and the whole evening changed for me. For he was the Philip I knew and after greeting his mother and Jason, he came straight to me as if our conversation and parting had never taken place.

He stopped to pour out a glass of wine for himself and looked across at me.

"You're not taking any, Rachel?"

"No, thank you. I don't really care for it."

He stood in front of me, his eyes twinkling.

"So what did you do with the glass I sent you last night to drink to our future?"

I coloured nervously.

"I did sip it and drank to us, Philip, but it was so bitter I could not finish it."

"Yet the glass was empty."

"I'm afraid I emptied it behind the fire," I said guiltily.

He shook his head at me, and pulled up a chair to sit beside me.

"Naughty Rachel! It's good to be home again."

"You would have a cold ride."

"Yes, and an unnecessary one."

"You saw Miss Ainsworth?"

"No, she is away from home. Still, I did what Thea wanted and such virtue ought to be rewarded because I would much rather have stayed with you."

I smiled at him happily, glad that whatever had made him vexed with me had been forgotten, but before I could speak Thea asked plaintively:

"Well, Philip? Aren't you going to tell me what dearest Elaine said?"

"Dearest Elaine was not at home. She has gone to London for a period. I left your note, however, and they will send it on to her."

She frowned.

"You need not have left it under those circumstances. By the time she comes back all our plans may be altered."

"True," Philip said lightly, but with a meaning glance at me. "We will have to point that out to Elaine, if she tries to hold us to our invitation."

"You had invited her to come here?" Jason asked.

"Just to a family dinner to meet Rachel properly. I told her it would be a very quiet affair as we are still in mourning."

"Then you'll be glad she cannot come, no doubt," he replied in his usual brusque way and I saw her lips tighten in annoyance.

"Philip," I said, drawing his attention back to me. "I must tell you. When I came in I found my riding habit laid on my bed. Lizzie must have brought it while we were in the garden."

"Have you tried it on?" Jason asked.

"Yes, and it is a perfect fit. Now I will be able to go riding again. Philip, do you still mean to take me out?"

I turned again to Philip with that question and saw a very peculiar expression on his face. Suddenly it was the face of a stranger, yet the next moment he was smiling, again the charming and gay Philip I knew.

"Of course I do, Rachel. We will go tomorrow. We will ride up to the high moor and, if it is clear, I will show you the view from the top."

"Take care it is not too far for the first time," Jason said sharply. "Remember she hasn't ridden for many years."

"But it is not a thing one forgets," Thea said.

"Perhaps not, but then she rode astride. Now she must go side-saddle. Quite different, don't you agree?"

"Yes, but Philip will take care of her. You won't be afraid with him, will you,

Rachel? He won't allow you to take risks, even if you want to."

"No indeed. How could I be?"

I smiled at Philip and saw that Jason was frowning and wondered why. Then I thought that perhaps he was annoyed because I was not going out with him for my first ride, but I shrugged that thought off, determined that I was not going to give up my appointment with Philip.

Yet when he spoke it was apparent that this was not his motive, after all.

"Enjoy your ride, Rachel," he said, "but don't forget there are some old mine workings up there, so try not to gallop like the wind."

"As if I would! I hope I know enough not to run before I can walk."

"Splendid. I only wish I could come with you, too, but I have a very busy day before me tomorrow."

"We wouldn't dream of keeping you from your business," Philip said, smiling at me. "Would we, Rachel?"

"Of course not. Anyway, I trust you to take care of me, Philip."

"Thank you," he said and his fingers

closed on mine for a brief delightful moment.

Mrs. Ramsden came in then to tell us our meal was ready and while we ate we talked only of generalities. When the last course had been served, Thea pushed her plate away and said wearily:

"Philip, I am sorry, but I am in great pain."

He pushed back his chair and got up at once, his expression concerned, as indeed it might be because she looked very drawn and white.

"Why didn't you tell me before this? What a brute I am not to have looked after you better. Shall I carry you or will it hurt too much?"

"I can bear it, I think, and Anna knows exactly what to do."

"Come along then."

He lifted her gently and her face twisted with the pain of it. Then he said quietly to me:

"I'll see you in the morning, Rachel. I won't leave Thea until she is comfortable once again."

"No, Philip! I don't want to spoil everything for you."

"Do you think I would enjoy myself, knowing you were suffering? Come, let us brave Anna. She is going to be very annoyed with us both, I'm afraid."

I watched him carry his mother carefully out of the room and thought how good he was to her. A good son, so it was said, made a good husband, and if that was true then my future should be a happy one. Though for the first time the anticipation of the time when Philip and I would be man and wife did not bring the thrill of delight which I usually felt.

But perhaps that was because I was tired and just a little bit scared of the morrow. Because as Jason had said, it was a long time since I had been on a horse and then I had ridden astride like a hoyden. And although it must be a joy to be out alone with Philip, it was a joy which was mixed with a great deal of trepidation.

I got up on that thought and said to Jason who had been regarding me thoughtfully:

"I think I will go to bed now, to be ready for tomorrow."

"Yes, do that, it would be wise. Do you still bolt your door?"

"Yes. It is very cowardly of me, isn't it?"

"Not at all. The press is still against the panel?"

"Yes. No one has moved it."

"Good." He pushed back his chair and got up. "Come along, and I will light your candle for you."

He held out his hand and after a moment's hesitation I put mine into it. And as our hands met I felt a sharp sensation run up my arm like a quivering live thing, as if I had touched something ardently vital, and my fingers tightened convulsively on his.

I could feel the pain of that grip yet it did not hurt but only produced in me a kind of wild excitement, an excitement which seemed to pass from my hand into his.

His eyes burned down into mine and I felt as if I was enclosed and up-held in a fiery circle.

Then suddenly he flung my hand away from him and went quickly out of the dining-room into the hall and lit the candle standing on the table by the stairs, leaving me standing, bereft and confused, my breast heaving as if I had been running very fast. Then slowly I followed him.

He waited until I reached him, then handed me the lighted candle and said, without looking at me:

"Goodnight, Rachel. God bless you and keep you."

"Goodnight," I answered as well as I could, then went slowly up the stairs. When I reached the top I stopped and looked down at him. He had not moved and I felt a sudden wrench of pain at my heart. Because he looked so sad and lonely, standing with his head bent, one hand covering his eyes.

I wanted to run back to him, to pull his head down against me and caress away the trouble which was so apparent in his attitude. But I knew I could not, and after another moment I went along the passage to my bedroom. There I sat down on the inglenook seat and thought with a shudder of what my reception might have been if I had given way to my impulse, because Jason Holcroft could be curt and cutting without any such reason.

Nevertheless, as I prepared for bed I could not help wondering what his reaction might have been, and I had to concentrate very hard on Philip and my ride with him on the morrow in order to push the thought of Jason out of my mind.

14

MEG helped me to dress next morning and when I was ready clasped her hands together and said:

"Oh, Miss Rachel, you look beautiful. Mr. Philip'll be proud to take you out with him."

I smiled gratefully at her for to be truthful I needed some reassurance. Because I was feeling very nervous indeed and could not think how I would go on. Philip was used to riding with Miss Ainsworth, who I was sure was magnificent on horseback. I hoped he would not be too bored at having to take me out with him. I could not help saying as much to Meg.

"Thank you, Meg," I said, "but he's used to riding with Miss Ainsworth and you know how well she rides and how lovely she is. If he compares me with her—"

"Then he'll have to admit you're best.

Why, she's just pretty, Miss Rachel, but you're beautiful. Eddie thinks so, too." Then she added anxiously, "You'll not go through that place where the old mine is?"

"No. Mr. Philip said he'd take me on to the moors, but whichever way we go, I'll be quite safe with him."

She shook her head obstinately.

"I don't know about that. It's a bad place, Miss, that it is."

"You're being silly, Meg. You know I don't really believe in ghosts and things like that. Besides, I shall be so busy trying to stay on the horse, I doubt if I'd notice a ghost if it stood up in front of me."

Meg lifted her hands in horror.

"Eh, don't say such things, Miss Rachel, even in fun! They don't like you to make mock of them."

Later, when I went downstairs to join Philip, I told him what Meg had said, expecting him to laugh about it, but instead he took it as seriously as she did.

"It's better not to joke about the supernatural, Rachel. I have a healthy respect for it. Thea has always believed in ghosts. She's seen them, too."

I shivered uncontrollably, as if a goose had walked over my grave.

"I should hate that. Thank goodness it can't happen to me. I'm much too down-to-earth."

"That's true indeed," he said, and although he was only agreeing with what I had said myself, I felt unreasonably annoyed.

"Shall we go?" I asked, quite sharply for me when speaking to Philip, and was immediately ashamed of myself. Was I to fall out with him because he had told me the truth as I knew it myself, and because he had failed to admire me in my new outfit? And as I went with him to the stables, I tried to overcome this queer mood of dissatisfaction with him.

The horses were saddled and ready and the grooms were leading them round the yard when we arrived. Philip's big roan and a smaller dun-coloured mare for me.

"This is Dulcie," he said. "Come and be introduced."

I stroked her tentatively and she threw up her head nervously, then nuzzled against me.

"I've had Thea's saddle put on her for

you. She'll never need it again, I'm afraid," he sighed.

"Never, Philip? Is there then no hope of a recovery in time?"

"None," he answered, then added more cheerfully, "come, I'll put you up and the groom can walk you round the yard while you get the feel of the horse and saddle."

At first as we circled the yard at walking pace I felt very strange indeed and much inclined to grasp at the mare's mane. But gradually I became more confident and gave Dulcie the office to trot.

She did so and after two or three more rounds the groom released the bridle at Philip's shouted instruction and I took her round a few times myself, before reining her in and looking down at Philip triumphantly.

"Well done, Rachel! You'll do!"

I turned my hot but smiling face to him as he swung himself on to his roan, and said:

"You admit then that I'm not an absolute tyro?"

"I do. I can see I shall have to look to my laurels. Shall we go?"

"I'll get my horse, sir," the groom said.

Philip's mouth hardened.

"I don't think we shall need you, shall we, Rachel? Are you willing to entrust yourself to me?"

"Of course, Philip." I smiled down at the groom. "Thank you for all your trouble, but we shall do very well on our own." But I was aware of him standing watching us as we went out of the yard, his face a mask of indecision.

"I do not think he cared for us going out without him," I said.

Philip shrugged.

"He's Jason's groom and thinks he owns the stables. I shouldn't trouble about him."

"No, of course not," I agreed, and said no more for we had now left the grounds and were beginning to climb. And although I had done well enough in the yard, it was taking all my concentration to ride the mare.

Then we reached the top and Philip's horse broke into a canter. Dulcie followed suit and for the next few minutes until I managed to rein her in, I felt as if I was being shaken about like a sack of meal.

Philip wheeled and trotted back as I stopped.

"What's the trouble, Rachel?"

"Nothing," I answered breathlessly. "It's just that I don't seem to have got the proper rhythm yet."

I was sitting facing in the opposite direction to him and as I looked beyond him I saw the tall figure of the gypsy woman suddenly appear at the edge of the moor.

My fingers tightened involuntarily on the reins and Dulcie almost shied as I cried:

"There she is again!"

Philip wheeled his horse round.

"Who? I see no one."

"I thought I saw the gypsy but you're right. She's gone now. Perhaps it was only a shadow," I added slowly, because the appearance and disappearance of the woman had been so swift, and the clouds crossing the weak sun were making deep shadows on the ground.

"Let us get on then."

I set my horse in motion, determined this time to keep her to a decorous trot and Philip waited for me to pass him, before falling in slightly behind me. We rode along in that manner until I suddenly realized that I had at last, quite unconsciously, dropped into the correct rhythm.

I started to turn my head to tell Philip this when I sensed rather than saw something flail through the air. I jerked forward automatically and felt a stinging blow across my shoulders. At the same time Dulcie leaped forward, taking me completely by surprise and the reins were wrenched out of my loosened grasp.

I grabbed her mane, holding desperately to it, because she was galloping now and I felt as if my head was about to be torn off at the roots. I gasped out a little prayer, because I knew that unless she stopped soon I could not hold on much longer. My fingers were already numb and I was being flung about so that the breath was jerked out of my body and my arms felt as if they would be pulled out of their sockets before very long.

Then I heard hooves thundering behind me and knew thankfully that my prayer had been answered. Philip was coming to my aid.

I had a flashing vision of his big roan as it passed me, then there was a sharp crack and Dulcie reared up on to her hind legs. Then she brought her forefeet down in a way which jarred me through and through.

I felt my fingers loose their hold and then, as she went into the air again off all four feet with arched back I was tossed over her head and saw the ground coming to meet me.

I came struggling out of a deep blackness into an awareness of throbbing pain, opening eyelids which seemed to be weighted down and trying to focus a tiny point of light which seemed to move and sway as I strained to hold it in my vision.

Then I saw no more as I was engulfed once again into the darkness.

When I awoke the second time I knew immediately where I was and though my arm ached badly, it was bearable, as was the daylight which filled my room. I turned my head on the pillow and saw Meg sitting by the fire, her head bent over some sewing.

"Meg," I said, and was surprised by the tiny sound my voice produced.

She jumped up and came to me, her face wreathed in smiles.

"You're awake at last, Miss Rachel. We were beginning to think you'd never open your eyes again, so we were, even though doctor said it was only the knock on your head was keeping you asleep."

"Knock on the head? Meg, what's the matter with me? With my arm."

Because as well as feeling the dull ache in that member, I could see it laid across the bed, all bandaged and stiff.

"Don't you remember? Well, doctor said you wouldn't at first and we weren't to let you worrit yourself about it but just tell you right away you fell off that dratted horse."

"A horse!" I echoed, immediately rejecting that explanation. Because if I couldn't remember how I came to be lying in bed with an aching head and arm, I knew I hadn't been on a horse since I was twelve years old.

"Yes, but stop worriting about it. I'm going to give you some milk and then the cordial the doctor left for you to have as soon as you woke up. Now I don't want to hear another word out of you till you've drunk it."

I did as she ordered and, indeed, was

glad to, for the strain of the few words I had exchanged with her made my head begin to throb wickedly.

When she laid me down on the pillows again I closed my eyes against the light which had begun to trouble them and tried to focus my mind on what she had said. But the words slid away from me as I tried to catch them, and I must have dropped asleep almost immediately.

The next time I was aware of anything there was a lamp burning beside me and Mrs. Ramsden was sitting beside the fire, fast asleep. I did not disturb her because now my head was clear and my memory no longer confused.

I put up my hand and felt the bandage around my temples, then explored the area of the other arm stretched out on the top of the quilt and realized for the first time that it was kept stiff by boards. It must then be broken, I thought, and in the same moment knew again the fear which had shot through me as the horse leaped under me and I went flying over her head.

"Philip!" I said aloud and Mrs. Ramsden woke with a start and blinked over at the bed.

"You've waked," she said in a pleased voice. "How are you feeling, my dear?"

"Better," I said. "Much better."

"Good. Now I'm going to prop you up so that you can drink the chicken broth I've made for you. Doctor said you'd probably wake tonight and be ready for it."

"I don't want anything," I told her peevishly, then was ashamed when she said:

"But I made it special for you. The stock was so thick you could stand a spoon straight up in it, and now it's all wasted."

"I'm sorry, Mrs. Ramsden. Of course I'll have it."

"That's a good girl. You'll feel the stronger for it, that you will."

I drank all the broth and after the first few mouthfuls found I was enjoying it. Nevertheless when she said she would give me the cordial the doctor had left, I was adamant in my refusal.

"I won't have it. Not yet. It'll put me to sleep again and I want to know what happened."

"But Mr. Jason said—"

"I don't care what he said. I've got to know. Please tell me, Mrs. Ramsden."

"I daren't do that. Mr. Jason wants to tell you himself."

"Then bring him here."

"It's near two o'clock in the morning, Miss Rachel. You can't get him out of his bed now."

"I don't see why not."

"When he's hardly had a decent night's sleep since you fell off that horse? Shame on you, Miss Rachel."

I moved my head restlessly.

"But I've got to know."

"And so you shall, come morning. I'll bring Mr. Jason to you just as soon as you've had your breakfast and I've neatened things up a bit. You wouldn't want him to see you now, all mussed up like you are."

"No, I wouldn't," I said, surprised at the strength of the feeling that when Jason came I wanted to look as well as I could. "Give me the cordial then."

"There! Now when you wake up tomorrow you won't know yourself, you'll be so much better."

And she was right. I was hungry for the breakfast she brought me soon after I awoke and even the effort of being washed and helped into a fresh nightgown and wrapper did not tire me too much.

I waited for Jason to come with a fervent anticipation, yet when he did so, walking quietly into the room, I could find nothing to say to him. He stood beside the bed and smiled at me.

"So you've wakened at last, Rachel. I was beginning to wonder if you ever would."

I managed to find my tongue.

"I'm made of sterner stuff than that," I said tritely. "How long have I been ill?"

"Almost a week," he replied quietly.

I stared at him, trying to assimilate the knowledge that I had lost a week out of my life, that I knew nothing of what had been going on around me during that time.

Jason brought a chair up to the bed and sat astride it, his arms resting on its tall ladder back.

"Can you remember what happened?" he asked.

I nodded, then winced at the stab of pain which shot through my head at the movement and I saw his lips tighten.

"It was Philip," I whispered. "He

struck at me with his whip and Dulcie took fright—"

"He hit you? Then the doctor was right. He said that was a whip lash across your back. I'd like to—"

He said something under his breath which I did not hear, his brows as black as thunder, and I said quickly, in an effort to reassure him and to get things clear in my own mind:

"I don't think he intended to hit me. He meant it for Dulcie but I got in the way. I realize that now."

For I did realize it and for the first time, gaining strength from this steadfast man, I faced up to the truth my mind had refused to acknowledge. That Philip, who had said he loved me, had deliberately incited my horse to run out of control, knowing I was too inexperienced a rider to recover.

I waited for the inevitable pain which that knowledge must bring with it, but I felt nothing, nothing but a kind of wonder that he should have thought it necessary to do such a thing.

"The gypsy was there, too," I said

suddenly remembering. "I saw her just before—"

"I know she was. She was watching over you, Rachel, at my request. It was she who gave the signal which brought me to you just in time."

"You?"

"Yes. I saw you thrown by your horse and managed to prevent Philip from administering the final coup de grâce."

I stared at him with suddenly dry lips. "I don't understand," I breathed.

He got up and strode across the room to the window, looking out through it, his back to me. Then after a moment, as if in that time he had come to a decision, he returned to me, looking down at me with pity and taking my uninjured hand in his.

"This is going to be very painful for you, Rachel, but you must face up to it if you're to have any happiness in the future. Face up to it and overcome it."

My fingers tightened on his.

"I know it," I said firmly.

"Then you remember what happened?"

"Yes. I couldn't do anything to stop Dulcie. Then I heard a horse galloping towards me and I thought Philip was going to stop her, but instead—"

"Instead?" Jason repeated quietly. "Say it, Rachel. It is the only way."

I took a deep breath.

"Instead he struck her again and she threw me. I went flying over her head and the ground came up to meet me."

I closed my eyes and drew a long shuddering breath, yet even as I felt again the fear that terrible moment had brought to me I knew Jason was right. In recounting it to him, it had already begun to lose some of its terrors.

I felt his hands warm and hard around mine and was grateful for their comfort, clinging to them as if to a life line.

"I saw you hit the ground," he said at last. "Those few minutes as I galloped towards you, praying you had not been killed, were the longest in my life. But I was in time, thank God."

"In time for what?"

"To prevent Philip from finishing what he had begun. I wrested the crop out of his hand as he raised it to bring the handle down on your head."

I shuddered and closed my eyes, still clinging to his hand.

"I'm sorry, Rachel. I know how much it must be hurting you to know that Philip tried to kill you."

I opened my eyes then, looking at him with complete surprise. Because in that moment of truth I knew he was wrong. It was not Philip's perfidy that was filling me with horror but the fact that if he had succeeded in his purpose I would not now be lying in my bed with my hand in Jason's, lapped in his strength and care. Though I was not yet ready to follow that thought to its conclusion. Instead I said with a gasp:

"Why, Jason? Why should he try to kill me? And those other times. He wasn't responsible, was he?"

"Not directly. That was Thea."

"That's impossible. She can't walk."

"Yes, she can. Apparently she's been able to for a long time but it suited her to continue to play the cripple. That way she didn't have to be a true wife to Tobias," he finished bitterly.

"You mean she pushed me into the ha-ha and tried to suffocate me?"

"Yes."

"And you prevented her," I said slowly. "How was that?"

His hand moved in mine but I held on to it tightly.

"Having brought you here where I suspected there might be danger, then I had to take care of you, Rachel."

"You—guarded me. Thank you, Jason." I was silent for a while, then said as the thought occurred to me, "And Meg?"

"That too was Thea. You see I had told Meg not to let you out of her sight. I don't think they intended to harm her really, but only to immobilize her so that you hadn't a companion to make things difficult for them."

"I see," I said slowly, and indeed I did, though it was a different picture from that painted by Jason, and I shivered as I thought what might have happened if Meg hadn't screamed and brought Eddie crashing through the trees to her. Perhaps she would not have been sent plunging to her death down the old mine, but I was not convinced.

"Thea was the headless woman?" I asked and he nodded.

"Yes. She took advantage of the old superstition that the mines are haunted."

But I was hardly listening to him because I was horrified by a fresh suspicion.

"Jason, do you think—Grandfather—?" I stopped, unable to put into words what I suspected, but I had no need to say any more. The grief on Jason's face was sufficient to answer me.

"I don't understand," I said at last. "I suppose I can see that Grandfather—if Philip thought he was the heir, but he would have got it one day. Why couldn't he wait?"

"Because Tobias was beginning to be suspicious and Philip needed money and position because he'd fallen in love with Elaine Ainsworth. He knew her father would never let her marry him, even though he might inherit one day. Because he couldn't be sure."

"I see." I stopped and swallowed hard, then went on bravely, "I see why he had to—pretend he loved me to get control of everything, but why didn't he wait till Mr.

Lacey had done all the legal matters before
—before trying—"

He laid his hand gently against my
cheek.

"Because he couldn't if he was to win
Elaine. You see, her father refused to
allow her to meet him any more because
he was no longer eligible as a husband and
he couldn't bear the thought of losing
her."

"Poor Philip."

"You can still say that after what has
happened? Rachel, if only—"

I waited for him to finish the sentence,
then when he did not, asked, "If only
what, Jason?"

"Nothing," he said quickly. "Only I
should have realized the lengths to which
he and Thea were prepared to go."

"But I don't properly understand. Even
if I—were no longer alive, would they
have benefited?"

"Yes, because although Tobias didn't
make a new Will, he did add a codicil to
his old one many years ago, and Thea
knew of it. She also knew that your grandfather was having second thoughts about

making Philip his heir and had threatened to disinherit him."

"But he died before he could do that?"

"Yes."

That one word was spoken with such sorrow that it was a while before I felt able to intrude upon his feelings. Then I asked quietly:

"What did the codicil say, Jason?"

"Everything was left to Philip, his adopted son, apart from specific legacies embodied in the Will, if your father was dead and had left no legitimate issue."

"So I had to die before I could make a Will."

"Yes."

I closed my eyes, thinking over what Jason had told me, trying to understand it, to accept it. But I found it quite impossible.

"I can't believe that Philip would be so —so dreadful."

"Don't blame him too much, Rachel. Not that I'm excusing him, but he was not the real villain in this case."

"You mean—it was Thea?"

"Yes, it was Thea."

"You said she wasn't really crippled

unhappy. Lying here I've had time to think. I know now that I let myself be carried away by what seemed like a childish dream come true. I thought to fill the void left in my life by Mama's death without stopping to ask myself if what I felt was true love."

His fingers tightened upon me.

"What are you saying, Rachel?"

"I'm trying to tell you I never loved Philip. I loved a dream, a vision." I paused, knowing that there must be nothing but truth between myself and this man. "I was crying because you would be leaving me now there was nothing to keep you here and I hated the thought of that."

He looked at me, his eyes brilliant with hope, and I looked steadily back at him, willing him to believe me even though it hardly seemed possible that he would do so after the manner in which I had treated him. But I need not have doubted.

"Rachel," he murmured at last. "My dearest love."

And as his lips touched mine, gently at first then with increasing passion, I knew

but was only pretending. Did Philip know?"

"He did, but not until after Tobias died. The only person who knew Thea had recovered from the bad toss she suffered was Anna, her maid. She is devoted to Thea and would do anything she wanted."

"I'm glad Philip didn't know. Did Thea admit being the headless woman?"

"She didn't admit it but I think she caused Tobias's death in the same way as she tried to bring about Meg's."

"But—she must be mad!" I said, appalled by his words.

"No, just obsessed. Obsessed by love for her son. He must be given everything he wanted in this world, and he wanted Miss Ainsworth. When no answer was received to Lacey's advertisement, she was sure Philip would inherit. Then you came on the scene."

"I can see it must have been a shock."

"It was, though I'm sure then they did not mean you harm."

"But you warned me not to come here. To take care."

"I thought they might trap you into marriage against your will and make you unhappy. If I had kept quiet about the Trust, perhaps none of this would have happened."

"Oh, no, Jason, you mustn't blame yourself. It was not your fault. Thea—and Philip—must have been very wicked." I clutched his hand tightly. "Jason, I don't want to see them again."

"You won't, my dear," he answered gently. "They've gone. They left the day we brought you back here after the—accident."

I breathed a sigh of relief.

"I'm glad. I wouldn't have wished to—"

I moved my head on the pillow and felt the tears gather in my eyes, though I could not have told why I was crying. Perhaps it was for a dream in which for so short a time I had looked forward to a lifetime of happiness, to no more loneliness.

Instead I had to face the fact that I was on my own again, not friendless, it was true because I knew I could count Jason as my friend. But he would go away, also, back to his own home for there was nothing now to keep him at Clifton Manor. And at that thought the tears spilled over and rolled down my cheeks.

Though I was not crying for Philip for the loss of my dreams. I was mour because Jason would be leaving me a would be bereft and desolate.

Then I felt his hands on my shoul gripping me tightly, hurting me be in his eager intensity he had forgotte broken arm.

"Rachel, don't cry. I can't bear i isn't worth it. Please believe me darling. He isn't worth one mon unhappiness."

I opened my eyes and looked in face, hearing his voice calling n darling, all the rest lost in the joy two words had raised in my heart he was speaking again, saying word I could hardly believe.

"Rachel, I love you. Oh, I know stand a chance, only I want you now, that one day when perhaps y last forgotten Philip, I'll be wai hoping."

I put up a wavering hand and his face, feeling that touc through my fingers with a shocl delight.

"You're wrong, Jason.

that I had indeed come home. Through fear and danger to the haven and joy of Jason's love.

THE END

We hope this Large Print edition gives you the pleasure and enjoyment we ourselves experienced in its publication.

There are now more than 2,000 titles available in this ULVERSCROFT Large print Series. Ask to see a Selection at your nearest library.

The Publisher will be delighted to send you, free of charge, upon request a complete and up-to-date list of all titles available.

Ulverscroft Large Print Books Ltd.
The Green, Bradgate Road
Anstey
Leicestershire
LE7 7FU
England

GUIDE
TO THE COLOUR CODING
OF
ULVERSCROFT BOOKS

Many of our readers have written to us expressing their appreciation for the way in which our colour coding has assisted them in selecting the Ulverscroft books of their choice. To remind everyone of our colour coding— this is as follows:

BLACK COVERS
Mysteries

*

BLUE COVERS
Romances

*

RED COVERS
Adventure Suspense and General Fiction

*

ORANGE COVERS
Westerns

*

GREEN COVERS
Non-Fiction

ROMANCE TITLES
in the
Ulverscroft Large Print Series

THE SHADOWS
OF THE CROWN TITLES
in the
Ulverscroft Large Print Series

The Trial of Charles I   *C. V. Wedgwood*
Royal Flush   *Margaret Irwin*
The Sceptre and the Rose   *Doris Leslie*
Mary II: Queen of England   *Hester Chapman*
That Enchantress   *Doris Leslie*
The Princess of Celle   *Jean Plaidy*
Caroline the Queen   *Jean Plaidy*
The Third George   *Jean Plaidy*
The Great Corinthian   *Doris Leslie*
Victoria in the Wings   *Jean Plaidy*
The Captive of Kensington Palace
    Jean Plaidy
The Queen and Lord 'M'   *Jean Plaidy*
The Queen's Husband   *Jean Plaidy*
The Widow of Windsor   *Jean Plaidy*
Bertie and Alix   *Graham and Heather Fisher*
The Duke of Windsor   *Ursula Bloom*

FICTION TITLES
in the
Ulverscroft Large Print Series

Enquiry	*Dick Francis*
Flying Finish	*Dick Francis*
Forfeit	*Dick Francis*
High Stakes	*Dick Francis*
In The Frame	*Dick Francis*
Knock Down	*Dick Francis*
Risk	*Dick Francis*
Band of Brothers	*Ernest K. Gann*
Twilight For The Gods	*Ernest K. Gann*
Army of Shadows	*John Harris*
The Claws of Mercy	*John Harris*
Getaway	*John Harris*
Winter Quarry	*Paul Henissart*
East of Desolation	*Jack Higgins*
In the Hour Before Midnight	*Jack Higgins*
Night Judgement at Sinos	*Jack Higgins*
Wrath of the Lion	*Jack Higgins*
Air Bridge	*Hammond Innes*
A Cleft of Stars	*Geoffrey Jenkins*
A Grue of Ice	*Geoffrey Jenkins*
Beloved Exiles	*Agnes Newton Keith*
Passport to Peril	*James Leasor*
Goodbye California	*Alistair MacLean*
South By Java Head	*Alistair MacLean*
All Other Perils	*Robert MacLeod*
Dragonship	*Robert MacLeod*
A Killing in Malta·	*Robert MacLeod*
A Property in Cyprus	*Robert MacLeod*

MYSTERY TITLES
in the
Ulverscroft Large Print Series